Trader:

A History of Trade

David F. Palmer

i

Linellen Press
265 Boomerang Road
Oldbury, Western Australia
www.linellenpress.com.au

To Laura, Miranda, Sally and Julian,

Family is wealth beyond measure.

Contents

A History of Trade

History is, to a large extent, the story of human conflict. But there is another aspect, perhaps even more pervasive, than the history of warfare: that is the history of human co-operation. This is particularly evident and largely well documented in the history of trade, the voluntary exchange of items of value between different groups and individuals, each seeking to enhance their own situation by peaceful means. The stories in this book are based on that theme. They are fictional, although some effort has been made by the author to place these imaginary events into a reasonably accurate historical perspective where ever possible.

The reader may find some aspects of these stories a little confronting, particularly some of the attitudes portrayed by some of the characters presented. But those aspects are intended to show conditions and norms as they are believed to have existed in the times and settings in which the story is told, rather than those which prevail today.

Flint and Shells - circa. 10000 B.C.

Gnog edged forward through the low waist-high scrub, his arms outstretched as he did so. As he progressed, he cooed a loud guttural urging: "Haa, Haa, Haa …" Off to his left about twenty metres, Gruug moved similarly, making the same noises. About fifteen metres off to Gnog's right, the female, Hurrah, also edged cautiously forward, her arms upraised to chest level as the scrubland canopy consumed more of her shorter stature. Her noises were higher pitched to reflect the smaller, more constricted windpipe of her proportionally smaller larynx: "Hai, Hai, Hai…"

The net was closing as the group moved closer to the startled fawn, panic now clearly settling into its mindset. It gazed apprehensively from left to right and back again, searching for an escape route through the shrinking cordon that was now enveloping it. Its panic was heightened by the realisation it could no longer escape its pursuers by merely bounding in the opposite direction from which they approached. The land it had traversed so swiftly in similar times of peril had suddenly disappeared. In its place was nothingness – just a huge void of space – the cliff before it plummeting away to the valley floor over fifty metres below.

There were nine in the hunting party. Gnog and Gruug were the largest – the two dominant males of the group – although it was still largely unsettled as to who was the stronger. Hurrah, the mid-aged of the adult females, was the object of both the dominant males' attentions at times when hunger gave way to lust – usually at night around the cave firelight after the troop had eaten whatever food was available. The older female, Yayia, had been the male attention subject until a few months ago, her advanced state of pregnancy now lessening her appeal for the moment. She was currently well off to Hurrah's left, advancing slowly along the edge of the cliff-face, echoing the same high-pitch peal Hurrah was projecting. Moving along the right-hand edge of the cliff was the youngest of the fertile females, Whoora. She had yet to be accosted by either of the two dominant males, but each had already noticed her recent flowering. Her cries were even shriller than the other two adult females as she advanced in the ever-diminishing cordon midway between Whoora and Gruug.

Between Hurrah and Gnog were the young pre-pubescent male, Reenz, and his somewhat young sister, Treebi. They both proceeded with arms raised aloft as the scrub canopy scraped beneath their armpits and their necks strained to peer over the vegetation surrounding them. Their shrill cries mimicked those of their elders, although their progress was more cautious, even hesitant. Thirty metres to the rear of the enveloping semi-circle were the two remaining party members, the diminutive male, Seetai, the top of his head barely visible above the bushes. Holding his hand was the even tinier baby of the group, the almost naked female Miav. She trailed along after the boy, almost totally oblivious to the drama unfolding ahead.

The semi-circle tightened. Only five or so metres separated each of the converging humans. The fawn had nervously backed further out onto the promontory into which it had been driven. The scrub cover had fallen away and it could clearly see the plunging cliff falling away from an ever-increasing arc to its rear. Its mouth started to froth as its rapidly accelerating breath dragged ever-increasing quantities of oxygen into its lungs, drawing sustenance to fuel the energy burst its instincts dictated it would soon need to make.

The seven pursuers emerged from the scrub almost simultaneously, only a few metres separating them now. Gnog glanced right, then left, gesturing as he did for the rest of the group to press ever closer to the terrified animal. As the fawn edge backwards, its rear hoof slipped on the crumbling cliff edge. It scrambled to regain its footing; it succeeded after a short struggle. But it was of little respite. The converging humans were only metres from it now, and there was scant room between them through which to dash. The fawn edged back further. It slipped again, scrambled frantically, this time unsuccessfully. It disappeared from view almost like magic.

Gnog and Gruug edged closer to the cliff-face and peered down. They could clearly see the grotesquely distorted posture of the fawn on the rocky valley floor below. They could clearly see the crimson splashes of blood around its quivering outstretched legs. The fawn raised its head weakly, trying hard to command its shattered body to rise and flee. But the body would not respond. And the head just reclined and rested on the rock. The eyes of the fawn glazed over and stared into nothingness.

It took Gnog and Gruug half an hour to descend the cliff. They had to backtrack about a kilometre to the ravine, both knowing from previous hunts where they could descend from the cliff ledge to the valley floor, albeit at considerable risk. They did not wait for the rest of the group. Speed was of the essence now – they had to get to the stricken deer before a scavenger, human or animal, discovered it. The men needed to reach it, guard it and claim it as their own else the whole group's hunting efforts would be in vain. The women and children were not vital to this phase of the hunt, so it was not imperative they keep up on the descent. They could descend at a more sedate and safer pace. It was the men who must now make haste, risk or not.

Luck was with them. No interlopers found the meal before they arrived to secure it. They quickly set to work to skin and butcher the carcass.

Gnog commenced work, proceeding in the time honoured way, slashing the fur with a roughened edge of a rock chipped from local granite. It was repetitive, laborious work requiring the repeated scraping of the rudimentary tool over the same portion of the surface, working until the outer layer exposed the pink skin beneath. But Gnog was used to the task. He had done it countless times before. He knew it took over an hour to skin and dismember a carcass fully, even a small one like this. However, as he worked, he became aware that Gruug, working at the hind end of the beast, had moved from the hoof of the hind quarters to the rump and that his slashing motions seemed much more effective and penetrating than Gong's.

Gnog paused to observe his brother. The latter worked on unaware of the attention of his sibling. Gnog leaned forward and watched Gruug's cutting action closer. His initial observation was immediately confirmed. Gruug was penetrating the fur and exposing the pink skin beneath with unusually few strokes. Gnog abandoned his position at the head of the carcass and moved closer to Gruug. He grunted.

"Cut fast," he observed in a guttural tongue barely differentiated from gurgling sounds.

"New knife," replied Gruug.

"Cut quick," reported Gnog.

"Hhmm," grunted Gruug.

"Let see," demanded Gnog.

Gruug paused and looked at Gnog, unsure if he should.

"Let see," demanded Gnog again, this time in a more insistent tone.

Gruug edged back, anchoring his toes into a rock crevasse as he did so. Gnog's tone sounded threatening and he was not sure if he was soon going to have to defend himself and his new possession. He pondered the situation for the moment. Gnog was his sibling, but he was also his rival for the females and the food. Tests of strength were not common between them, but they were not unknown either.

Gnog waited. His demeanour was more inquisitive than demanding, or so it seemed to Gruug, so the latter decided he would acquiesce rather than refuse. He held up the thin wafer he'd been cutting with between his thumb and forefinger. Gnog scrambled forward to gain a better view. Gruug quickly withdrew his hand, wrapping the small flint knife in the palm of his hairy hand as he did so.

"Let see," asked Gnog again, this time with a touch of pleading curiosity in his tone. Gruug obliged by placing the edge of the knife on the fur where he'd been cutting before Gnog had challenged him. He made a single purposeful stroke, revealing as he did so a neat incision through the fur, which fell away neatly to reveal the pink skin beneath. Upon completing the stroke, he looked back up at Gnog, making sure he palmed the knife as he did so.

"Me see," proclaimed Gnog, clearly showing some sense of excitement. "Me see," he pleaded again.

Gruug performed the cutting task again on a portion of the

skin higher up the leg.

"Me see, me try," clamoured Gnog, edging closer to his colleague.

Gruug considered the request. His rival was not showing any signs of aggression in his request, merely excitement and curiosity. Gruug decided to grant the request. He handed the small flint knife to his sibling. Gnog stroked it gently. He tested the sharpness with the thumb of his left hand as he held the knife, sharp edge uppermost, in his right hand. Then he leaned forward and applied the blade to the fur surface of the deer carcass before him. He slashed again across the same spot, then again in quick succession. To his amazement, he was through in just three strokes. Normally he would have expected a dozen or so. Then he sat back on his haunches and examined the tool.

"Where from?" inquired Gnog.

"Upland," said Gruug.

That was Gnog's first introduction to flint tools. It came as a total surprise to him. He had never seen anything like it before. From that day forth, Gruug rose in his estimates considerably. Gruug knew where the wondrous artefact had come from, and Gnog wanted to know too. But whenever he asked about its source, Gruug only shrugged and flicked his head in the general direction of the mountains far to the north.

It took Gnog a further three weeks to extract from Gruug how and where he had come into possession of the flint knife. And his enlightenment came at considerable cost. The young female Whoora had been attracting increasing attention from both senior males over the period. The tension between the two was steadily mounting as to which of the two would attain first access to her.

It would have come down to a confrontation to settle the matter – possibly a physical one in the normal course of events. But Gnog's persistent questioning of Gruug about the source of the knife, together with his insinuations that he was prepared to negotiate the sharing of this knowledge, had finally resulted in an implied proposal – if Gruug divulged the source of such treasures, Gnog would not contest access to the young female further.

Execution of the contract came one dark night in late September as the group huddled around the fire in the cave after a somewhat meagre meal of small adolescent wild boar. As both males finished their respective portions of the smallish beast's two hindquarters, each began to eye, firstly Whoora, and then, more suspiciously, each other. The intention of each was quite clear to the other even if the somewhat pre-occupied young female's attention was elsewhere. She was busy trying to extract the last vestiges of nourishment from the paltry remnant of the meal to which her station in the group had entitled her.

Suddenly Gnog sensed the time was right to seal the bargain on access to the girl. He moved carefully around from his side of the fire to a spot next to the wary Gruug.

"Where find cutter?" he asked bluntly.

Gruug blinked and looked back at Gnog, somewhat surprised at the half-menacing, half-conciliatory tone of his interlocutor. He stared intently for a few moments into Gnog's dark eyes, searching for a deeper meaning to the approach. Then he glanced at the unaware Whoora and then back to Gnog.

Gnog nodded ever so slightly.

Gruug glanced back at Whoora again and then back to Gnog, this time focusing intensely into his brother's eyes. The latter nodded again, this time in a more pronounced and clearly affirmative manner.

Gruug paused to assess the offer. Then he leaned forward and said in a low whisper that he was sure that only Gnog would hear:

"Got Upland. From mountain men. Many moons' walk. More than toes many. Gave shiny shells. One hand big fingers many."

Then he jumped up and skipped quickly around the edge of the fire and grabbed the startled Whoora by the wrist; started pulling her towards the back of the cave. The young woman shrieked and pulled back, looking appealingly at Gnog to intervene. The young lad, Seetai, scurried quickly to his mother's side, and the stone-faced Yayia placed a protective arm around him and drew him near to her. As she did so, Hurrah scooped up the baby Miav and pressed it to her breast as she cringed unobtrusively back into the darkness beyond the glow of the fire.

Whoora shrieked again and called for help from Gnog. But Gnog casually leaned down, picked up a discarded trotter and began to gnaw on it. His gesture was unmistakable. The matter was settled; for Gnog, for Gruug, for Whoora and for the whole group. It was the natural way of things in their world.

Gnog set out three days later. All the following day, he had scoured the gently lapping shallows of the coastline near the cave and found six respectable-sized, well-conditioned conical Trochidae shells. This was the currency Gruug had indicated was the price of a flint knife. According to Gruug, only four were required, but Gnog felt it was better to have ample bargaining power with him just in case it was more or in case there was more than one knife to be had.

The second day after the fireside negotiations, he busied himself with provisioning for his trip. He goaded, bullied and cajoled the rest of the group into rising early for another hunting trip, though most were quite happy to rest for the day after eating their fill of the meal the previous night – the hunt had been successful in killing a small wild goat. Gnog settled for the forequarter of the animal, from which he had sliced a dozen strips of meat for his primary food source over the coming couple of weeks.

These he had taken the next day to a large rocky outcrop about two kilometres up the coast from the cave and spread out on a flat rock to dry for the day. As he waited for them to cure, he collected from the nearby promontory a fur bag full of wild pomegranates, returning half-hourly to check that his meat had not been tampered with. The fruit would further supplement his future diet.

Gnog departed at daybreak on the third morning, delaying only to fill his goat-skin water bag at the nearby stream. He headed directly for the largest of the mountains to the north. In his right hand, he carried a thick, two metres long stick. Around his waist was a wide belt of deer hide. Tucked into that, weighing about three-quarters of a kilogram, was a stone axe made from a doubled-over sapling, its head secured above and below with animal sinew. Slung over his back was a fur bag containing his fruit, meat and the shell currency.

Gnog did not know it at the time, but this would be the first of fourteen such expeditions he would make in the coming four years. By the last of these, he was carrying over two dozen shells each trip and bringing home not only flint knives but also flint spear-heads. More importantly, he brought back the knowledge of how to attach those spearheads to sticks, like the one he had traditionally carried to club his prey and to defend himself. This knowledge ensured he not only ate very well, but he also enjoyed many more young females than when he'd had to spar with Gruug for their attentions. Now they sought him out to share his abundant source of food.

But Gnog lived in a hazardous world. Not only was there the constant threat of being misunderstood by the other humans he met on his travels, but venturing far beyond his traditional hunting grounds enhanced the risks of meeting other challenges for which he was ill-prepared.

On trip number fifteen, he had been careless when negotiating the now-familiar upland pass. A hungry lion caught him unawares and unaccompanied by his usual hunting companions. On that day, neither his newfound technology nor his now considerable negotiating skills were of any help to him. On that day, Gnog became the meal that that particular dominant male enjoyed.

Pyramid – 2560 B.C.

Memnet barked the order, and the three steering oarsmen on the port side leaned on their oars to ease the ship to starboard and clear the vessel immediately ahead of the *Khadim Faraouni* (Pharaonic Server) at the loading dock. Simultaneously his Mate, Dido, barked a similar command to the steering oarsmen on the starboard side, and they promptly tugged on their oars to accentuate the turn. The sleek craft slid slowly into the broader reaches of Pelusium Harbour – if one could describe as such the small collection of wooden structures on this modest, though increasingly active, seaside village at the sea mouth of the most eastern channel of the Nile Delta.

Toward the middle of the vessel, sixteen slaves, sitting two abreast down the centre of the ship, pulled leisurely on each of their oars, eight port side and eight starboard side, to power the ship forward.

In the cool morning air, both officers and crew – bonded and free – attended to their respective tasks with diligence and quiet temper, since all expected this would be a productive and rewarding trip – albeit, of course, with significantly different expectations of their individual rewards. For Memnet, owner and master of the *Khadim*, this promised to be a most profitable trip. For Dido, likewise, since his sailing bonus would be generous if it was so. For the overseer, the three under-overseers and his four guards, it would also be financially rewarding. For the slaves, it would be a light-duty trip because the voyage up the Nile would be largely wind-driven, the port entrances and exits the only times real ardour or compulsion would be demanded of their physical labour. And for all, the food would be good; the rest plentiful; the weather mild, and the dangers from thieves, pirates and other malefactors would be minimal now they were under the full protection of the Pharaoh's army.

It had not always been so. In the days when Memnet plied the Red Sea trade from the Egyptian port of Wadi al-Jarf to the land of Punt, the slaves were much surlier and the pirates more aggressive. So too was the Levant trade north from Pelusium to Byblos where, in addition to rebellious slaves and aggressive pirates, you could never be quite sure if the Semites of Judea or the Phoenicians of the Cedar Coast would still be at peace with Egypt when you arrived in their waters. It was hazardous work but lucrative. Egypt lacked timber resources, so cedar brought high prices in the Nile port markets. The copper and turquoise mines of Wadi Maghareh and Wadi Kharit in Sinai were also very profitable.

But he had been young then and keen to show his dependability and reliability to his father and his uncles, who had built the fleet up fivefold since they had inherited it from their father. And he had done so, now being regarded as the natural heir-apparent as the family patriarch now his senior clansmen were ageing. But that promise was also tenuous. Memnet had seven other cousins. At least three of them were considered worthy contenders for the family leadership so any misstep could snatch the prize from his grasp.

But this departure did not appear to be the challenge that could unseat him. It was the start of a one hundred league trip (just over a thousand kilometres) up to Aswan, then a return via Giza to Pelusium. The prevailing wind at this time of the year was from the north, so most of the trip upstream would be wind-driven. The trip downstream from Aswan to Giza, and subsequently back to the sea, would follow the current flow and be relatively effortless.

From a profitability point of view, all that was required was for saleable and profitable cargos on both upstream and downstream legs. For the former, Memnet had secured a cargo of Lebanese cedar, much prized in the timber-starved upper reaches of the Nile, particularly for major building projects in Memphis, Giza, Luxor, and Aswan. This profitable bulk cargo was supplemented by two high-value, low-volume commodities, two double heqat (of 19.2 litres each) of Myrrh originally from the Indian land beyond the great ocean, and four thousand deben (just over fifty kilos) of lapis lazuli from Badakhshan (in Afghanistan).

For the downstream leg, Memnet had secured a two-year contract to supply casting stone from the quarries around the first cataract of the Nile around Aswan to the port of Giza. This was the finest stone in the land. It would grace the Great Pyramid's final surface the Pharaoh was building for his tomb and entry portal to the afterlife when the time came – which should not be long now because Khufu's time on Earth was drawing to an end – or so the seers were predicting. In between the interim ports of Memphis, Giza and Thebes, would be opportunities to pick up and discharge various grains, wheat and barley, and other opportunistic cargoes as space and spot markets permitted.

So, all up, it should be quite a profitable trip, and few – hopefully none – exciting moments, which might have stirred his blood in younger times but which he now, in his more responsible years, could well do without.

On the prow of the ship, a single eye painted on each side of the flat vertical bow sprit stared at the ribbon of water stretching away to the north and south as the craft cleared the harbour entrance. This time starboard-side steering oarsmen leaned on their oars, and their port-side counterparts tugged on theirs, turning the *Khadim* to the south and upstream.

"Hoist the sail," ordered Dido, and four of the central oarsmen handed their charges to their adjacent slave-rowers who pressed down on both port and starboard oars to hold their blades above the surface of the river as the ship glided slowly forward under its own momentum.

The sail rising was brisk and only a few minutes passed before the wind caught the upraised barrier and bellowed it outwards. The momentum of the ship quickened noticeably in the morning breeze. Then central oars were retracted and stowed along the length of the deck, leaving the ship entirely under wind power.

At eighty-seven *mahe* (royal cubits) in length (about 45 metres), eleven and a half *mahe* (about six metres) in width and just under four *mahe* (about two metres) in draft, *Khadim* could carry around thirty-three thousand *deben* (about 450 tonnes) of cargo with one and a half *mahe* (about four-fifths of a metre) of freeboard. The bulk of her cargo for the upstream journey was twenty-thousand *deben* of cedar wood and ten-thousand *deben* of emmer wheat. The latter was inferior to Egyptian wheat but still saleable to stingy slave owners and cash-strapped poor worker customers who could not afford the premium Egyptian grains that grew in abundance along the banks of the Nile. The Myrrh and Lapis were the icing on the cargo cake and took up very little space. This left *Khadim* with about ten per cent spare capacity for opportunistic cargos in

Avaris, Bubastis, Memphis and Thebes for transport to Luxor and Aswan.

The stone contract would provide most of the bulk cargo for the downstream trip, from Aswan to Giza port, at least, and after that Egyptian wheat pickups, as available, would be readily saleable in Pelusium further downstream and along the Mediterranean coast to Rafah and Gaza and all the way north to Tyre by the more seaworthy vessels of the family fleet.

Memnet felt well pleased with himself and his commercial arrangements as the ship entered mid-channel, and his personal servant appeared from the galley with beer and sweetmeats for his morning breakfast.

There was little opportunity in the lower ports to supplement the upstream trip to Memphis. As it turned out, though, Memnet took on ten vessels of olives from the Hellenic land, one thousand *deben* of malachite originally from Lidia, and eleven small strong boxes of electrum, originally from Anatolia – this had been marooned in Avaris when its original shipper had his vessel impounded by the local Governor for failing to pay outstanding fines imposed from his insulting the Pharaoh in a drunken outburst in a local portside beer hall. He sold three thousand *deben* of cedar wood and two thousand *deben* of emmer wheat at profitable but not spectacular prices.

But more valuable to Memnet was the passenger he took on board for the Heliopolis-to-Memphis leg of the trip. The man was in a hurry to get to Giza and was happy for a lift to Memphis from where he could easily hire a cross-river private courier to Giza port. He had begged Memnet to call in at the Great Pyramid service port on the way, but Memnet had assured him the family's contacts in Memphis could arrange for a more convenient and cheaper option for him than diverting the almost fully-laden *Khadim* to facilitate his crossing. Memnet also offered him accommodation in the family's villa in Memphis overnight as their guest. Though in a hurry, the stranger accepted, seeing Memnet's reluctance to divert and not being sure when a new travel opportunity might arise.

Memnet was not being entirely hospitable with this generous offer. The stranger was obviously a man of considerable importance in Giza, a valuable future contact and personal acquaintance for a Nile trader in the Great Pyramid construction city. It was contacts like this that had won him the casting stone contract in the first place.

It proved a shrewd move: the man was assistant architect to the great architect himself and, during the evening meal in Memphis, he revealed to Memnet that the next phase of the great construction project was the lining and covering of the Pharaoh's own future burial chamber – although, of course, he could not reveal exactly where in the structure that would be. But this phase of the construction required the transport of roof covering stones for the chamber, huge stones three times the length of the usual granite blocks from which most of the pyramid's interior was constructed. These were exceptional materials – unique, in fact – and they would require highly-skilled couriers to transport them. Hiring such contractors would require premium shipping prices which would be readily paid to the successful tenderer.

As the evening wore on and the talk became looser, the bond between guest and host became firmer, and the mutual confidence in each grew. Towards the end of the evening, the architect inquired if Memnet considered his firm would be up to the task. Memnet replied that he thought it was, given the family's long history in the Nile trade.

During final drinks, and over Anatolian fruiters' sweet delicacies, the two clasped hands in agreement. The stranger agreed to pen a letter of introduction to the Aswan quarries' chief stonemason, who just happened to be related to his wife's family.

The *Khadim* continued its upstream journey calling in at Thebes along the way. The Myrrh and Lapis had been sold in Memphis on arrival for the lucrative prices Memnet had anticipated when he'd taken those cargoes on board, and so had half the remaining cedar wood, also at a profit. No new significant trading or new cargoes were exchanged or acquired from then on, except for the remainder of the cedar, which proved readily saleable in Thebes at expected rates. Also, a few thousand *deben* of einkorn wheat from the minor ports along the way were welcomed by the quartermaster of the Aswan garrison for standard fare. *Khadim* arrived in Aswan relatively light in final load, which was quickly unloaded to local dockside market traders.

After a good night's sleep, Memnet headed for the nearby stone quarry's main site office and presented his letter of introduction to the chief stonemason. The balding, potbellied man examined the seal, nodded approvingly, broke it and perused its contents.

"You come well recommended," he muttered. "And at a convenient time too. Can you take delivery straight away?"

"My ship is awaiting your cargo," said Memnet confidently.

"What is her capacity?" inquired the official.

"Thirty-three thousand *deben* full capacity," said Memnet, "but its load utilisation depends on the shape of the cargo. How is your load distributed?"

"This initial load comprises six *mahe* slabs, each four *mahe* wide and one *mahe* thick," said the stonemason. "Each weighs six thousand *deben*."

Memnet baulked. Six slabs weighing six thousand *mahe* made a total load of thirty-six thousand *mahe* compared to *Khadims*'s rated capacity of thirty-three thousand *mahe*. It was only nine per cent over capacity, but it would mean a lower freeboard by about three-tenths of a cubit, which lowered the margin of safety. But the Nile flood was largely dissipated in its flow at this time of year, and it would be clear water all the way to Giza. With no significant navigation hazards to negotiate along the way, the overloading seemed to carry only minor risk compared to the lucrative nature of the cargo.

"I see no impediment to accommodating that," Memnet said confidently.

"Fine," said the stonemason. "The cargo is on the Eastern Dock at Pier Three. You can begin loading at first light tomorrow. See my scribe for the despatch authorization."

And with that, the two shook hands, and the stonemason withdrew to his inner chamber.

Memnet returned to the *Khadim* and briefed Dido who would attend to the loading. He then retired to the luxuriously appointed owners' inn and supped for the night before retiring early.

Memnet slept well, rose early, ate a hearty breakfast then headed off for Pier Three. He was in good spirits. But that didn't last long. He was met at the head of the pier by Dido, looking decidedly distressed.

"Sir," he said, almost breathlessly, "I don't think we can carry this cargo, not all at once, anyway."

"Why?" queried Memnet. "It's only a little over our rated capacity. The river is quite calm at this time of the year. All we have to do is just drift with the current."

"It's not the weight," said Dido. "It's the shape. All six of these blocks are one solid mass, each a huge mass. We can't distribute the weight to optimize the distribution of the load. And because they're rectangular, their four corners are wider than the narrowest sides of the ship below decks. To accommodate them, they will have to be carried above the deck, stacked one on top of the other, six high."

"So?" queried Memnet.

"It raises the centre of gravity," explained Dido. "Instead of it being below deck, below the waterline even, it will be above deck, three cubits above deck to be precise," he said. "That will make the ship hugely unstable. One strong gust of crosswind would be enough to tilt her a few degrees, and if she tilts even that much, with such a small freeboard, that could dip the gunnels beneath the surface. And once she does that, once she starts shipping water, she will lose buoyancy almost instantly. She will literally sink like a stone."

"Nonsense!" blurted Memnet. "You're being alarmist, Dido. You know I usually trust your judgement but I think you're overreacting to the possible hazards. There is no reason why we should get a sudden crosswind at this time of year. The wind is steadily north-south this time of year. You're being over-cautious."

"Yes, sir," replied Dido, "but the river is not straight. There are many twists and turns between here and Giza. There will be many times when the wind will cross our bows and even some when they are across our midships. One strong gust on those occasions and she could tip."

Memnet trusted Dido's judgment and had to concede there was such a possibility, one he had not considered when he'd accepted the contract. He had only considered the overweight issue. Load disbursement, or rather more particularly, the cargo distribution's indivisibility, had not occurred to him. Now it did.

"We're locked into this contract now," he said. "It will cost a fortune to get out of it. Is there anything we can do to reduce the risk?"

"We could load the cargo in vee-shaped formation, with three slabs side by side, stowed down on the floor of the cargo deck. That would lower the centre of gravity to about waterline level. But we will have to take up the deck to do so. We could store the deck timbers as secondary cargo for the trip and rebuild the deck at the end of the trip. It would take a day to lift it and another to reinstall it at the end. And some timbers would probably be damaged in the process and might need to be replaced. We could do it, but it would be expensive."

Memnet swore under his breath. No wonder the stonemason had offered a premium price to carry this cargo. He probably could not find another carrier who was prepared to do all that. Nor could he have found a larger vessel to carry this cargo. *Khadim* was one of the largest ships on the Nile run as it was. This wily stonemason had obviously been aware of this since he received the order to carve these roof slabs.

But the cargo was prestigious, and the family's reputation rested on delivering on its contract, so Memnet had little choice but to do what was necessary. The contract did not look quite so lucrative now. It might even result in a loss on this leg of the trip.

Memnet delivered on the contract. The roof slabs arrived in Giza intact and on time. The whole exercise resulted in a small loss on the downstream leg that rendered to whole round trip only modestly profitable.

Memnet was now an even wiser Nile trader than before,

and he now had a valuable lesson to pass on to his subordinates and successors: Make sure you know all the terms and conditions of the contract, both the legal obligations and the physical constraints before you enter into any contract.

Blood Money – 178 A.D.

The oars dipped into the calm surface of the Mediterranean Sea as the trireme edged its way along the coast in a northwesterly direction. Soon it would round the point two kilometres ahead then straighten up into a more northerly direction, and run adjacent to the continental coastline. Split was still three days rowing from here. It would take all of that time and the exhausting effort from the galley slaves lining its three decks if a more southerly wind did not resume in that time. That was not likely at this time of year. The hot, dry Sahara breezes did not usually start until late July or early August. The slave market, or more accurately, the premium prices of the early summer sales, would not wait for the vagaries of nature. No, brute human effort was the only thing that would ensure profitability on this trip so the overseer's lash would have to be applied liberally in the coming days and nights.

Marcus Vestus Galba would normally have been quite relaxed at this point of a Black Sea trading venture. The trip out from the Italian mainland usually involved a cargo of olives, wine and weapons. These items brought good prices in the Dacian coastal settlements markets and from Provincial Governors, who especially appreciated a good vintage. They also needed the swords, pila, shields and body armour to equip their latest batch of reluctant recruits into their local militia centuries.

But Marcus was not relaxed on this trip. He was facing a substantial loss on this trip if he could not get good prices for the slaves this vessel carried. He had made nothing on the outbound leg of this voyage. His trading in Constantinople had been fair and had yielded sufficient recompense to cover the fit-out and provisioning for the round trip. That was normal and expected. But he had expected to make a profit on the Black Sea leg of the voyage, and a good one too. He needed to. Provisioning in the colonial ports was outrageously expensive, particularly manufactured supplies that had to be shipped from the Italian or Greek ports. There were local manufacturers, of course, but the Dacians were not renowned metal workers, and most of what they provided was substandard. To buy their manufactures was to risk breakages at sea, which could be disastrous.

Two days out of Constantinople heading north along the Thracian coastline, Marcus' trireme, the *Esther Matriarch* — named after his mother — had been attacked by Thracian pirates. Three swift sail-boats, each with twenty or so men on board, had loomed out of the darkness. Their crews boarded her a few hours before dawn. Surprise had been almost total. The coastline had, supposedly, been secured by the Roman army and fleet these past forty years, so it was the last thing any seasoned sailor — or his equally seasoned guard commander, Quintus Sextus Commodus — would have expected. In fact, both were fast asleep at the time of the attack. Only the slave overseer and his two drivers and their whip hands, coxing the skeleton rowing teams at a leisurely pace, were on duty. The guard sergeant was on the poop with two Greek guards, and the shift guard commander, a young blond lad with fuzz rather than stubble on his chin, plus two more Greeks, were on the forward castle. The pirates had come in silently, converging tangentially from the port and starboard bows. Fifteen to twenty intruders were on the main deck before the alarm was even raised.

To their credit, the fore and aft Roman officers had leapt into action as soon as they realized what was happening, but the inexperienced boy on the bow was dispatched with merciless ease. The veteran sergeant on the poop was overpowered by the Thracians, two who grabbed him by the arms whilst a third quickly and ruthlessly disembowelled him. The other four Greek guards gave no such heroic service – the unfairness of the fight was readily apparent to them. Two immediately leapt overboard; the other two grounded their weapons and stood back with arms outstretched to the heavens.

The rest of the crew also gave little resistance. The steersman simply stood his ground, gripping the steering oar and staring dutifully, if not somewhat nervously, ahead. The slave overseer tried to apply his whip but his soft weapon was no match for the Thracian warrior who challenged him. The former was quickly dispatched. So too were the slave drivers on the second and third decks. Their fate was doomed no matter what they did. Slave drivers were the most hated of all Roman servants and were given no quarter by any of Rome's enemies.

The rest of the guard had little chance to defend the ship either. They were all asleep below when the pirates boarded, and the intruders were upon them even before they could arm themselves. Those who reached for their swords soon dropped them when menaced by the overpowering Thracians

– sensibly so, as they were in a confined space. Although they could defend their quarters, it was a worthless citadel given it was cramped, without provisions and with no other exit than the doorway the Thracians dominated.

The slaves in the ship offered no resistance either, not that they could be expected to. The rowing detail was chained to its oar station, and the off-duty teams were locked in the slave hold. There was nothing any of them could have done even if they had wanted to help defend the ship. Not that many of them would have wanted to, of course. Most would probably have joined the attackers if they had been able to.

Even so, despite the sudden attack, its decisive outcome and its financial loss, Marcus had been lucky in the encounter. He had not needed to fight – it was all over by the time he exited his cabin. And it was immediately clear to him that any resistance on his part would have been suicidal. So he composed himself as best he could, drew his toga about his frame with an air of regal superiority – or so he hoped it appeared and simply demanded, in his most imperious voice: "What is the meaning of this?"

A tall, fierce-looking man, clad as a gladiator, stepped forward and responded with a hearty laugh. "You, my friend, have been chosen to support the Thracian people with your generosity. And given the puny response of your military escort, I'm sure you will not deny our request for alms."

"I most certainly will!" retorted Marcus, again summonsing up his most pompous gesture and trying to keep the quiver from his voice.

"Indeed?" said the Thracian in a menacing tone. He stepped to one side and motioned those behind him to move forward. Three men did – two Thracians dressed in armored battledress stood either side of a disheveled Quintus Sextus

Commodus. The eyes of the latter were wide with fear, his face ashen grey. The hapless Roman soldier had no time to speak. The Thracian pirate leader placed the blade of his sword on Quintus' exposed windpipe and sliced it swiftly back towards his body. Quintus' eyes bulged even wider. A gurgle emanated briefly from his mouth, followed by reddened foam. Simultaneously blood gushed from the open wound on his neck and flooded down the front of his white toga. The two escorts released the sagging body of the dying Roman and let it slump to the deck.

Marcus said nothing more for the next four hours. Not much was said by others either, save for the curt commands of the pirates as they supervised the transfer of the cargo to their vessels.

No other blood was shed that night. There was no need. The pirates were clearly in control, and debating or resisting would only have brought death.

When the cargo transfer was completed, just as dawn was breaking, the pirate leader turned to Marcus and said:

"Remember, Roman, this night I have given you your life. Live well and long, but do not sail these waters again".

Then he vaulted over the side of the ship into his last remaining boat and disappeared towards the still darkened eastern shore of Europe.

The pirates had not released the slaves on board the *Esther*. They clearly did not need men for their rebel army. Perhaps they thought it might buy them some clemency if they were ever caught by Rome again. Marcus should have been grateful for his reprieve from death – but he was not. There would be other voyages to Dacia, although next time, his ship would be better armed. For now though, the priority was to get to Split.

"Pick up the pace, Dracus," he ordered the new slave

overseer he had recruited at the Danube outpost. "We have to make better time than this."

Dracus picked up the pace to four knots, rotating the rowing team every three hours instead of the usual four. By morning the *Esther* was just over one hundred nautical miles from Split. Dracus reported the ship's progress to Marcus at the dawn watch change over. But he also counselled:

"The rowing slaves are approaching exhaustion. I don't think we can drive them at this pace for much longer. About half of them are close to breaking. I think we should slacken off the pace a bit."

"No," said Marcus. "We must get into port by sunrise tomorrow or we'll miss the last sale of the week. If we do, we'll have to wait until after the feast days that the emperor schedules for the end of each month. By then, the Egyptian and Moroccan traders will be in port and the slave prices will crash. We must get this load to market and sell them before the market closes this week."

"We may not make it at all if we keep going like this," said Dracus.

"Alright," said Marcus. "Take an extra shift from the field hands among the trading stock and blend them into the rowing teams. That will give you an extra rowing shift so you can spell each rower for a double rest period. That should keep them going."

"That will knock off some of the condition in the trading stock," said Dracus.

"Two or three shifts each shouldn't affect them too much," said Marcus. "They'll lose more value if we don't make the market than we will if they look a little tired. We should be in port within a day or so. A bit of work won't hurt them. It might even enhance their salability if we can show that they're still in good shape despite a day or so of hard labor."

The *Esther* made port by 10.00 am the following day, so Marcus had his trading stock on the auction block in time for the afternoon slave sale, the last for the week. But he didn't have it all his own way: a southerly breeze had sprung up as the sun had set the previous evening. It had added an extra two knots to the ship's speed, which had aided the timing challenge of the inbound trip. Unfortunately, it had also aided the speed of every other ship on the Adriatic that evening, so, by the time dawn broke, there were three sails to aft of the *Esther* – two of them slavers. One was from Naples with a cargo of field hands from the Tribune Casca's southern vineyards, now being redeployed to the general's Croatian estates. Since the latter was smaller than the source estate, half were auctioned to pay for the transport costs and the general provisioning of the vessel for the return voyage.

A second ship was a slaver from Tripoli with a cargo of slaves from the Niger Delta region. These had been transported across the great sea of sand by the cloth-headed merchants who had descended from the escapees of the sack of Carthage centuries earlier.

Both slave cargoes provided strong competition to Marcus's unskilled stock, whose physical condition was already degraded by Marcus using them as galley slaves.

But it could not be helped. Had Marcus not used them, he could have missed the sale entirely, given that the wind stiffened in the unexpected way it had. He had no way of knowing what was happening far to the south, even as his Egyptian and Libyan competitors were benefiting from its stimulus before him.

Marcus' stock fetched enough revenue to cover the cost of

the inbound trip from Constantinople and sufficient to provision the ship for the next outbound voyage. There was not an overall venture profit to the Galba household, however, so all up, the entire venture had been in vain.

Not all was gloom, though. The emperor, Marcus Aurelius, had heard of the Thracians' rebellious activities and was determined to remedy their insolence. He was also planning a major campaign across the Danube with the 14th and 17th Legions, and a massive military build-up was underway in Split and across the northern Italian provinces. Marcus' small fleet of three triremes had been commissioned by the campaign commander, the emperor's son General Commodus. The *Esther* was immediately provisioned and loaded with pitch, stone shot and rope to support the land offensive across the Danube.

Imperial cargoes always paid well, so the next voyage was likely to be very lucrative indeed. Also, legion troops would guard the cargo. The emperor did not want military supplies falling into the hands of his rebellious adversaries. If the Thracian pirates tried to repeat their insolent assault on a Roman trading vessel, this time, they would be in for a very nasty surprise.

Silken Road – 934 A.D.

The herd had taken the northern Tarim route of the Silk Road that ran from Kashgar through Aksu, Kucha and Korla, through the Iron Gate Pass, on to Karasahr, Jiaohe, Turpan, Gaochang and Kumul. It was now on the final leg of its journey to Anxi. There, Abdulweli hoped to trade the three hundred horses for silk to sell back in the Kashgar marketplace. It would fetch lucrative prices from the traders who plied the Silk Road further west, into Afghanistan and Persia.

But they were not at their journey's end yet, even though the most hazardous part of the trip was behind them. They had done well to get this far in such good order and had made the military checkpoint established by the now-deposed Tang Emperor without being disrupted by the Kara-Khanid Sultan's officials or challenged by any of the wild mountain horsemen or desert tribes along the way. That strategic bottle-neck on the great trade route was a perfect place for bandits to descend without warning and drive off large swathes of the herd before the vanguard or the rear-guard of the column could respond effectively to their raid. They had seen a couple of such bands on the hilltops in the distance, both before they reached the gate, and after as they had approached Tashidian, the first significant city beyond the pass.

They had been lucky this time. The bandits had not

descended. No doubt their small cavalry escort had deterred the would-be raiders, although that was only twenty men strong, and had only stayed with the herd to the limit of the Sultan's territory. They were now in the realm of Jingqiong, the new Khan of the Ganzhou Uyghur Kingdom, and it was more likely that it was his interest in the size and quality of their Uyghur horses that had deterred them. The new Khan's wrath would be great if this much-prized merchandise was disrupted. The bandits could easily evade any pursuing force, but their families would not be so agile if the Khan decided to inflict a lesson on precocious hill tribes who dared challenge his dominance of this particular section of the vital trade route.

The entire region had been in a state of flux since the Huang Chou rebellion had been put down fifty years earlier, in 884 AD. Since then, numerous kingdoms and multiple dynasties had risen and fallen, and there seemed no end in sight to the chaos. Every merchant plying the Silk Road had heard the horror stories of the great massacre of foreigners that had taken place in the Guang Prefecture in the fall of 879 under that rebel's bloody reign – a death toll ranging from 120,000 to 200,000 Persians, Arabs and Jews, so it was rumoured.

Further west, beyond Kashgar, over the mountains in the land of the Tajiks and further south in the land of the Afghans, the emperor's influence was very slight, even scorned. Their kinsfolk in the Tarim Basin tended to adopt that same contempt for their former Chinese overlords that their brethren to the west displayed. Even with a military escort, you could never be quite sure that you were safe along that stretch of the road even if it carried the patronage of the Sultan in Kashgar. In that realm, it was rumoured that his son,

Prince Satuq, had converted to Islam. His father was far from happy about his conversion, so even that Turkic realm was in a great state of flux.

Abduweli shielded his eyes as he gazed cautiously back towards the setting sun. With no dust on the horizon, nor specks on the hillside to the northwest, nor vegetation of any note on either side of the road, he felt reasonably sure the worst was behind them. The challenges that lay ahead would be more a verbal joust than a physical confrontation. But even then, he would need to be alert and nimble. The Chinese traders in the Anxi market-place had been at this horse-trading business for decades now, and they were well-skilled at getting the best deal possible for their master.

Then there was the weather that still had to be coped with. For now, it was calm, but the east wind had blown through the high narrow valley formed by the Qilian and Beishan mountains, reaching great intensity at its peak. It had unnerved the herd. The narrow pass through the Great Jade Gate still lay ahead, and the mob was still skittish. As they moved through the Hexi Corridor and into the Gan Prefecture towards the kingdom's capital Zhangye, Abdulweli hoped it would settle down. The last thing he needed was a stampede this close to journey's end. He turned his gaze towards the east and the road ahead and noted the growing darkness in the eastern sky.

"Make camp," he ordered. The ground was good here and the sooner he settled the herd, the better.

"Post a double guard tonight," he added to his order. The worst might be over, but Shunhua Khagan had died last year, in 933, and Jingqiong had only just succeeded him. Therefore, the royal line in the kingdom was still being bedded in and, since the last years of the Tang, large groups of bandits, some the size of small armies, still ravaged the countryside. Most were illicit salt smugglers, but they were known to ambush merchants and convoys, even besiege walled cities, so they would not be averse to rustling a herd of horses. Better to be safe than sorry. Even then, the new escort was a mercenary one and its loyalty and reliability was largely an unknown quantity.

The night passed without incident but Abdulweli was still up before dawn, hurrying the herdsmen and their Muslim overseers to hasten with early morning prayers and breaking their fast. He wanted to pass through the Yumenguan gate and on to the market-place as soon as possible. The herd was quite large by local standards and would attract considerable attention as it approached the market. He would pause its progress about three leagues out from the main square and hurry on ahead to announce its arrival. In particular, he wanted to alert the Khan's Horse Master of its arrival and elicit his early interest. If he could sell the whole herd in one neat transaction, he could then turn his attention to the task of buying silks for his return journey.

Initial inquiries via his forward emissaries had sounded encouraging, but a firm deal had not yet been struck. Abdulweli was aware that he was not the only western horse trader en route to this market – he was aware of two others approaching, one from the north-westerly prefectures around the Oocho Kingdom and another from the more northerly Dzungar Basin. The first deal done would likely be the most profitable. The arrival of the other two rivals would likely result in a downward price bidding war.

Abdulweli had been a trader for most of his life. As a child of seven, he had accompanied his father and uncles on Silk Road trade missions. He was well aware of the value of both local knowledge and an appreciation of the more significant geopolitical situation in cross-border trade negotiations. He thought his sources of relevant commercial knowledge were amongst the best in the land.

He was wrong. He lacked the one thing that his next potential customer had: the ability to compel informants to share their knowledge. All Abdulweli could do was offer money and other material inducements. His customer could actually inflict physical pain – sufficient pain to loosen even the most stubborn tongue. Getting the upper hand in these negotiations was primarily a matter of just how ruthless the inquirer was. In that contest, Jingqiong was unsurpassed, and so was his Master of Horse.

The latter's endeavours had revealed that potential buyers were en route to Anxi from the Karakhnid, and Ghaznavid Khanates too, and also from the rump of the deposed Tang dynasty now residing in the East, but which still craved their return to lands from which they had been ejected just a few decades earlier.

Abdulweli knew of the two other herds approaching Anxi that might present competition to his dealings with the new Khan, but he was not aware that he was not the only potential buyer. The other local Khans posed a serious threat to the new Quanzhou ruler – they would be even more so if their cavalry were to become a match for his own.

Jingqiong had instructed his Master of Horse to make sure that they would not be. His instructions to his minion were to buy up all and any Uyghur steeds that might be available in the local market, irrespective of the price. To comply with his master's instructions, the master horseman would have to act fast before his competitors arrived.

To Abdulweli's complete surprise, as soon as the faithful servant had completed his initial circuit of the resting mob, the entire herd was snapped up, at a most agreeable price, by the Khan's Horse Master. After a month and a half of hard worrying travel, the whole transaction was over in less than half a day.

Abdulweli spent the next few days roaming the Anxi marketplace, viewing and assessing the various offerings available, noting, in particular, the silk offerings for sale. He bought a few camel loads but, overall, he was not greatly impressed with the quality of merchandise. It had clearly been well picked over by other traders before he had arrived.

On his fourth day after his herd sale, to his surprise, the Ghaznavid caravan arrived. It now offered fresh silk stock, which was much more to his liking. Fortunately, the Oocho horse herd had also arrived the day earlier and had been snapped up by the Khan's Master of Horse in much the same manner as his herd had been. And the prices paid had been much the same as those he had received. The downside to this latter arrival was that there was now greater competition for the newly arrived silk stock, so the haggling started to heat up. Fortunately, it only lasted a day or so because, two days later, the Karakhnid silk caravan also appeared. It also carried a substantial level of silk offerings along with a good supply of fine porcelain. There was now a glut of silk in the Anxi market-place, making it a 'buyers' market for silk but still a very competitive one for porcelain. A day later, the Dzungar horse herd also arrived, significantly boosting the selling price of Uyghur horses as the newly arrived Chinese traders competed with the Horse Master for the now fairly sparse horseflesh offering.

The Master of Horse took the trade, given his master's uncompromising instructions, so the Dzungar traders enjoyed both higher prices for their horses and lower prices for their silk and porcelain purchases.

Ultimately it was the Chinese traders who came out worse off. Not only was their profit margin much lower due to lower selling prices for their silk and porcelain wares, but they were now without the horses their imperilled customers further east craved. But at least Abdulweli enjoyed the benefit of the now oversupplied silk stocks, so he was not entirely dissatisfied with the trading outcome. In trade, timing is everything.

Abdulweli left Anxi ten days later at the head of a caravan of thirty-four two-humped Bactrian camels, which better suited the cold climates of Central Asia, Mongolia and China, and were commonly used on the eastern trade routes. In Kashgar, he would on-sell them for breeding with their single humped Dromedary camels that were better suited for the western routes of the Silk Road. Kazak camel breeders would cross the two species, producing a bukht-hybrid, which was stronger than either of its parents. Each beast was laden with fine silk yarn, carefully packed porcelain and exotic spices from the lands beyond the fabled Great Eastern Sea.

On the eastward leg of this round trip, Abdulweli had enjoyed the protection of the Kara-Khanid Sultan's cavalry, to the border, at least, but from then on to Anxi he was dependent upon mercenary forces for his protection. The Jingqiong ruler had shown little interest in the west-bound trade, especially when it was Chinese and Muslim merchants plying it. So once again, Abdulweli was dependent upon mercenary forces for the caravan's protection. They were superb Uyghur horsemen, and their fighting qualities were legendary, but foreign traders could never be quite sure where their loyalties lay. As soldiers for pay, they often lay with the highest bidder.

All was fine until they passed once more through the Great Iron Gate and headed west out into the Taklimakan Desert. Eight nights into that crossing, their cavalry escort suddenly disappeared: when the caravan had bedded down for the night, the horsemen were there – at daybreak the next morning, they were gone, leaving the bewildered cameleers and their merchant masters staring anxiously at the barren plains all around them, and at the distant snow-capped Tien Shan Mountains far off in the distant north.

There was nothing Abdulweli could do but press on, doubting a return to the military outpost behind them or to any of the cities further to the east would result in any more a reliable escort than that which had just deserted them. They were on their own, defenceless.

Disaster struck two mornings later. As the sun peeped over the eastern horizon, a loud thundering boomed in the still darkened landscape to the west of the camp, and a band of around fifty horsemen charged into the still stirring space. The first charge went straight through the gaps in the tented campsite. The hapless, yawning souls who stumbled into the morning air felt the slash of a curved blade slice open their unprotected flesh. Their terrifying howls rent the air as the assassins dashed past. That the attack was well planned was obvious. The cantering horde's leftmost wing paused to slash the tether ropes and hoof-nobbles of the sedately slumbering camels at the camp's periphery. Within seconds, the once docile beasts were also cantering off to the east, herded by the rustling raiders.

The remainder of the strike force, now only about forty in number, drew rein in the distance in full silhouette of the rising sun. They raised a cloud of fine dust as it did so, then turned their steeds once more to the west. Each rider gave his mount a sharp dig in the ribs, and all beasts lurched forward together. Again the raiders slashed as they charged through, and again anguished cries arose from bewildered victims who had now emerged from their slumbers and their fragile tented protection. This time a dozen or so men went down.

By now, it was clear to all what was happening. The two dozen survivors still standing gathered their wits and what weapons they had stashed under their bedrolls. They formed up as best they could in a small circle about twenty paces in diameter in the centre of camp and prepared to defend themselves. Two had spears; seven had swords; the rest had little more than wooden staffs and knives. But they were not soldiers – that's what the cavalry had been for. But the cavalry was long gone; it was probably amongst the turbaned, face-covered horsemen that now confronted them.

The raiders did not charge a third time. This time they returned at a trot, then at a walk, then it slowly circled the caravan survivors forming an outer ring to the huddled group. They stopped, faced inward, weapons at the ready. A single horseman nudged his steed forward and addressed the cowering band of grim-faced defenders.

"You have a choice," he said in a Turkic dialect heavily laced with a Karluk accent. "The Book of Rights proclaims that we should not murder defenceless men even if they do trespass on our land. You can walk away, either to the east or to the west, as you chose, but you must discard your weapons before you do, and you must take only water with you as you leave. If you resist further, we will kill you all now."

"We have the permission of the Great Khan in Kashgar," offered Abdulweli. "I can show you his seal on his safe passage permit."

The horseman sniffed, pursed his lips and spat on the ground to his right.

"That dithering fool does not rule us," he said. "His protection is of no use to you here. Look around you: where is he? You are alone, old man. I alone can save you now."

"Surely we can negotiate," pleaded Abdulweli. "We have many fine wares we can offer you."

"I have them all now," sneered the impatient horseman. "Choose now," he commanded. "Walk or die."

"Where can we go?" wailed Abdulweli.

"Where ever you choose," said the horseman. "I would suggest you go east. You should reach water in a few days that way. You will not cross the mountains to the north. That way is full of bandits. To the south is desert for hundreds of leagues and even more mountains. To the west, it will be a week's walking until you reach an oasis, that's if you know where to find one, and assuming you can carry enough water for such a journey. No. If I were you, I would go east from whence you came."

Then the raider stiffened in his saddle. "Choose now," he commanded. "I grow impatient with your whining."

"We'll go east," said Abdulweli to the mounted stranger. Then he nodded to his assembled compatriots. Gingerly, they lowered their weapons, then one or two more, then all of them, discarded them. Slowly they turned and slunk off to their tents to gather their water flasks.

What price value - 1212 A.D.

Ali looked east out of the tent opening toward the sun; it rose sedately above the dimming, craggy, snow-enveloped monoliths of the Tian Shan Mountains, emerging from its nocturnal transit through the waning night. The highest peaks stood in dark relief to the broad horizon where the glistening golden orb appeared as its centrepiece. The lower slopes were now a darkened hue of red and green irregular mosaic that would make this land stunning in full daylight in a few hours. The now blackened foothills would also emerge as the shrinking shadows of their towering backdrop gave way as sunlight crept over them. Then the snow leopards would rise to eat their fill of bharal (blue sheep) if they were lucky, and the night predators – the foxes and owls – would retreat to their dens and nests and surrender their unconsumed prey to the foragers of the day. The smaller and more vulnerable creatures like marmots, hares, and seed-eating birds would also emerge and, in turn, would become prey to their terrestrial hunters and to their winged counterparts, the hawks, falcons and eagles.

Ali had never ventured this far east before. His usual transit was from Samarkand in the Kazak south to his home in Tbilisi in the west. This was some five hundred leagues (about 2,780 kilometres) across the Karakum Desert skirting south around the Kopet Dag range and on into Persia, then along the southern shore of the Caspian Sea, up through the lowlands of Azerbaijan, along the Kura River Basin and onto his homeland in Georgia. He had seen mountains before, especially in his youth when he had travelled north from home to the foothills of the mighty Caucus Mountains. But the majesty of these eastern peaks held him in awe.

Ali had travelled this east-to-west and return route fourteen times since taking over the management of the Babadishvili family trading business. In centuries past, he would have been royalty, but those days were long past. Now his kin sustained themselves with commercial endeavours and had been quite successful in that vocation.

Ali had assumed the role of Trading Master when his father was injured by an obstreperous camel that had shattered his right leg. The old man now maintained the business accounts while Ali led the caravans to the east. This was his fifteenth venture eastward to the lucrative markets of Samarkand. The familiar and well-worn path would have been his route home this time had fate not intervened. That westbound leg had now become too risky, and he sought a northern passage home across the northern coast of the Caspian Sea. It was a significant detour, but at least he might get home with his load intact and not have to forfeit it to some greedy sovereign or ruthless bandit now the Kazak city's hinterland was in turmoil.

It had all been quite unexpected. In 1212, the city of Samarkand had revolted against Ala ad-Din Muhammad II's rule, the Shah of the Khwarezmian Empire. The locals had killed some 8,000 to 10,000 Khwarezmians living there. It was now rumoured that Muhammad was on his way to sack the city and that he planned to execute 10,000 citizens of Samarkand in retaliation. Every foreign merchant in the city was planning to leave, and quickly, before the Shah's army arrived. Ali was among them.

He did not doubt the rumours for a minute and had been in the vanguard of this exodus. Muhammad II was ruthless. He had captured Samarkand in 1207 from the Kara Khitai, and in 1210 had taken Tabaristan from Bavandids and Transoxiana from Western Karakhanids. He had pursued his expansionist policy and conquered Tashkent and Fergana from Western Karakhanids shortly after. The regions of Makran and Balochistan were wrested from the Ghurids and Atabegs of Azerbaijan, and the hapless survivors became his vassals in 1211. He finally completed the destruction of the Western Karakhanids in 1212. It was highly likely that he would not be gentle on any of his new vassals if they dared to challenge his rule. Best to leave now while the Silk Road to the east was still open.

Georgia was a long way away from Samarkand, on the opposite end of the Khwarezmian Sultanate, far to the west. But travelling west would be dangerous for a foreigner in these turbulent times. It would be best to go east and then north to the Uyghur Sultanate. From there, he could travel west over the steppe north of the Caspian Sea. It would be a long time before he could get home, but there was at least a good chance that he might actually make it. And, by all accounts, there should be good trading opportunities along that route. However, precisely what commodities would be available in the east, Ali was not sure.

His specialty was Georgian wine, and his usual return load was silk yarn. The latter would still be available in Kashgar, but whether he could secure a suitably attractive load of commodities in Samarkand to trade for it in the eastern city was largely unknown. He had never been that far east before.

In any case, he was not sure what sort of reception he might receive in the east since the Mongol Khan, Temujin, who some now called the Great Khan, Genghis Khan, had now seized those lands. In battle, he was reputedly ruthless, but some eastern traders had said he favoured trade. So Ali should be safe if he could get to Sinkiang then head west via a northern route home.

In any case, speed was of the essence at this precarious time, and Ali had no time to wait for a suitably lucrative commodity cargo with the danger so imminent. So he opted to depart without a commercial load and risk what fate may offer in his circular transit. He could travel sooner and faster that way and put as much distance as possible between his train and the approaching tyrant.

That was three nights ago. They had made good speed with his lightly-encumbered camels, covering thirteen leagues a day by travelling from dawn until well into the night. The previous night had been their first real pause since leaving and had been a welcome respite for beast and camel-puller. But cavalry could travel faster than a camel train, even a lightly burdened one, so there was still no time to tarry. Ali barked an order to rise, and the response was swift and efficient.

The train departed within the hour, a remarkably quick time given the load his camels carried was not an inanimate one. Rather this trip, his cargo was mostly human, a modest population of hapless individuals and their families who were as keen to leave Samarkand as he was. Of the thirty-odd camels in his train, Ali was transporting no less than fifteen families comprising each a man, a woman and, on average, two children, ranging from one to five youngsters in each, a total of sixty-one souls. This was supplemented by a further eleven solitary men, most of whom were merchants equally fearful of the shah's wrath as he was. Each individual pared up with another and shared a camel with any surplus children who could not be accommodated on its family's main beast of burden. This meant that most camels in the train carried two adults or one adult and two children. An additional camel was assigned to every four people to carry the passengers' personal effects, those precious items families felt they could not abandon to the marauding Khwarezmians when the invaders finally took Samarkand. This included merchants' precious trade goods whose livelihoods were tied up in the merchandise they peddled.

The passengers had paid well for the privilege of Ali's largesse. This eleven-league stage from Samarkand to Tashkent would be one of the most lucrative trips Ali had ever made, if they could reach their destination intact. They had been fortunate to date, but there was no telling how close their pursuers might be, or, indeed, whether the avengers of the massacred would try and follow. Perhaps they would exhaust themselves with their revenge and plunder of the ill-fated city, then celebrate their triumphs with the excellent wine for which it was famed. Perhaps they would not pursue its escapees. But then they might. Capturing the train would be a financial bonanza for bandits of all kinds, especially with the gold the merchants carried in their saddle bags, as well as their trade stock. It was best to keep going. With luck, the camel train would reach Tashkent by evening.

The train had not gone two leagues before a hurried camel drew up alongside Ali at the head of the three-abreast central column of the procession. A distraught looking man in his mid-forties shouted at Ali:

"We have to stop. We have to go back," the man pleaded

loudly.

"What?" said Ali. "What on earth are you talking about?"

"My daughter," gasped the man. "She's missing. She's not with the men who were minding her. She's been travelling with them since we started, but now she's not with them. I can't find her anywhere."

"I can't stop this train now," said Ali. "It would take hours to get it going again. And in any case, half of the Shah's army is on our heels. If we stop, they're likely to catch up with us. I can't put this whole train at risk for the sake of one child."

"But she is only three," said the man. "She can't survive out here on her own. She'll die if we don't go back for her."

"You can go back and look for her if you like," said Ali, "but you'll have to buy the camel you take if you do. I can't take the loss of a valuable beast just to cater for your parental negligence."

"I only need to borrow it for a few hours," protested the man. "I've already paid you for its use for the trip to Tashkent. This small deviation to its path will not damage the camel in any way. I've already paid for its use for the duration of this trip. I don't see why I should pay you more."

"Look," said Ali, "there is likely to be a whole army riding to catch up with us. If you go back, you're likely to run into them. And if you do, they're unlikely to treat you very kindly." Then he paused to consider his last remark. "They'll kill you," he added. "They've probably already caught up with the child by now anyway, so they've probably martyred her already."

"I can't just leave her," wailed the man. "I have to try. Are you not a father yourself? Would you not go back and look for a lost child? Any father would."

Ali drew his camel to a halt. The man did likewise. The woman and two children accompanying him remained silent, but the woman's face yielded a silent plea.

"It is harsh, I know," said Ali, "but I have responsibilities to everyone in this train. You can go back if you like, but I suggest that your wife and children dismount before you do. They can walk with the baggage train until you return." Ali paused to reconsider again. "The two small children can ride on two of the baggage camels," he added. "That's the best I can do."

"Alright," said the man. "I'll pay you for the camel as you ask, but you must agree to buy it back from me when I get back."

"Agreed," said Ali.

"Fine," said the man. "How much for the camel?"

"Fifty Byzantine gold hyperpyron," said Ali.

"What?" exclaimed the man. "That's outrageous. It's only worth a third of that."

"That's at the camel market in Samarkand," said Ali. "There are plenty of camels available for sale there on a normal day. But we are not in Samarkand now, and this is not a normal day. How many camels do you see available for sale here and now?"

The man hesitated. What could he say?

"None," offered Ali in response to his own question. "I have the only ones available, and I can't really spare any of them. If I sell you this camel, there is a good chance you will not return with it. I will be one beast down, and I will have to redistribute its load to accommodate its loss. The load will include your family, who I will have to assume responsibility for the remainder of this trip until we get to Tashkent. Fifty gold hyperpyron seems a fair price to me for what I am offering you."

A flash of anger spread over the man's face, but there was

little he could do about the situation. His choice was to abandon his daughter or pay up.

"Be sensible," soothed Ali. "I know the loss of a child is hard. I have lost children myself. Like you say, I'm a father myself. If the truth be known, the child is probably already lost. If she hasn't succumbed to the heat, then she's probably wandered off in the wrong direction anyway. It is unlikely you would find her even if you did go back. I'm sorry, my friend. Sorry for your loss. But you still have your other two children and your wife to care for. You should think of them now.

"Pay him," shrieked the wife. "Pay him. We'll be fine. Find my baby. Please. Please," she pleaded.

"Alright," said the man. "But you must agree to buy the camel back from me when I get back. Agreed?"

"Agreed," said Ali.

The money was paid, and the camel unloaded of both wife and children. Their meagre goods were redistributed to two camels in the baggage train with a child perched on the top of each. The woman took up station at the head of the lead animal in this duo and readied to move on the instruction of the camel-puller for that file. The man replenished his water container, mounted the unladen beast and spurred it into motion retracing the camel train's path. Ali urged his beast forward as soon as he received the gold and was back at the head of the train even before the man turned back.

The remainder of the journey to Tashkent was routine and uneventful. The shah's cavalry did not overtake the train, and all, except the missing man and his lost daughter, arrived intact and disbursed to such accommodation as they could find, either to home, with relatives or to paid accommodation as was their want. Wherever they went, they were no longer Ali's concern.

With no substantial cargo to sell, Ali set about planning the next leg of his homeward journey. Tashkent was full of promising cargo: silk yarn, silk tapestries, cotton cloth, jade and many other commodities that would bring good prices in Tbilisi at journey's end. He set about restocking his train.

Just before noon two days later, a knock on the door of the room in the caravanserai he had rented as his temporary work office broke his deliberations. He opened the door to be confronted by the man who had returned to search for his daughter. The man looked tired and dusty but otherwise appeared to be well.

"I've come to return the camel," the man said.

"And the little girl?" inquired Ali.

"I found her half a day after leaving you," said the man. "She was tired, thirsty and stumbling along but heading roughly in the direction we had travelled. She said she woke to see us all disappearing into the distance. Obviously, the men I had entrusted her to did not wake her. I have yet to find them," he added menacingly.

"Allah be praised," said Ali. "He is indeed merciful."

"The camel," said the man. "It is in fine health, and I'm here to return it and recover my money."

"Ah, yes," said Ali, "our agreement. I can offer you eighteen gold coins."

"What?" exclaimed the man. "You charged me fifty."

"Yes," said Ali, "but that was out in the desert where there was no camel market and in extraordinary times. Now we are safe in a city where there is a thriving camel market. You cannot expect me to pay more for a camel from you than I would have to pay for an identical beast just next door. Circumstances have changed. Value has changed. The price I offer you is fair given our new circumstances."

"That's thievery," the man protested. "You took advantage of my distress and that of my wife. You knew we were desperate. You took advantage of our love for our child. What you say is shameful. How dare to treat me with such contempt."

"This is nothing personal," said Ali. "It is merely business. Circumstances change, and so value changes. What I offer you is fair here and now. I mean you no disrespect."

The man's face reddened.

"And you will not reconsider?" queried the man.

"I'm afraid not," said Ali. "Eighteen gold coins is my price. I will not offer you more."

Ali never saw the khanjali leave its scabbard. Nor did he see the thrust of its strike, save for the very briefest flash as the blade momentarily reflected the morning sun on its trajectory from the man's waist to his victim's chest. He did not even feel the pain of its penetration as the razor-shape blade entered his left breast just below his ribcage and sliced upward through his flesh, piercing his heart almost in the centre of its lower chambers. Clearly, the assassin was an expert in its use, a fact previously concealed by his modest peasant dress and hitherto whining demeanour. With his speed of movement and light sprung gait, this man was a man with considerable and well-developed military skills.

But Ali had no time to ponder these newly revealed qualities. He was dead before his body struck the ground and sprawled out languidly in a grotesque posture.

The man sprang back with cat-like precision and assumed a defensive stance. But further action was not called for. The prostrate cameleer lay lifeless before him.

The man drew himself slowly up to full height and reassumed a casual bearing. Then he gobbed a mouthful of saliva and spat it accurately into the staring face gazing unblinkingly skyward. He grunted, turned briskly and strode away.

Junk – 1405 A.D.

"What on earth is that?" exclaimed Ohmar.

"I've no idea," said Ahmed.

"It's huge," marvelled Ohmar. "Why, it must be four times the size of this ship."

"Probably more," said Ahmed. "Look! There's another one. It's just as big."

"I didn't know that you could build anything that size," said Ohmar. "I've been sailing this ocean for the last forty years, but I've never seen anything as big as that before. Where do you think it's from?"

"Well, it's not from this ocean," said Ahmed. "I've been sailing this one for over thirty years, all the way from the Red Sea to Madagascar and from the Gulf Islands to Malacca. I would have seen one if they'd been anywhere around the Indian Ocean in that time."

"It's coming from the south," reasoned Ohmar. "Do you suppose it might be from beyond the Malay Strait? You know … from the Cathay land that's supposed to be to the east of there … from the other side of the Eastern Sea?"

"Maybe," said Ahmed. "Look, there's another one. Allah be merciful! There's a whole fleet of them!"

"Hard to port," shouted Ohmar, suddenly gathering his wits. He did not want to take the dhow into the midst of these gargantuan behemoths. The sails alone would steal all the wind and leave his vessel floundering in their wake. Also, he did not know whether they were friendly or not, and he prudently chose to be cautious until he knew more about them.

"Are they armed?" he quickly inquired of his mate. "Do you see any cannon? There seems to be a lot of people on board, but I don't see any fire weapons. I can see some spears."

"There doesn't appear to be," said Ahmed. "But that doesn't mean they haven't got any. Can we outrun them?"

"I think we're about to find that out," responded Ohmar. "Make for Malacca at all haste."

Given the size of the strange vessels, it was difficult for the two Arab traders to guess their speed as they ploughed through the calm waters of the narrow strait. Ohmar knew the temper of the *al-Tajir al-Bahr*, so the only way he was going to find out with any accuracy was in a line-ahead race with them.

But Ohmar was more interested in the safety of his ship, his cargo and his crew than satisfying his curiosity at this time.

The direct course to Malacca, his destination, would take him on an oblique line across and away from the lead monster's starboard bow. Doing this, he could make a reasonable judgment of time speed from his standard navigational estimates on his expert judgement of all things nautical. *Tajir* could make about ten knots on a three-quarter reach in a fair wind and was quite fast for ships that usually crossed the Arabian Sea and the Bengal Bay.

After half an hour of this oblique course, Ohmar could see that the *Tajir* was widening the gap between his quarry and himself so, clearly, his craft was faster than theirs. Although he was trying to achieve maximum speed, he was not sure whether they were actually trying or not. Quite possibly not.

Given their size, they would not fear anything currently plying this ocean. For all he knew, they could be just meandering. Either way, he was not hanging around to find out. He would sate his curiosity later once he had gained the safety of Malacca harbour, which, only being a few years established, had little in the way of fortified protection, but there was likely to be some ships and men in port that had firearms.

The alien fleet did not alter course to pursue him, however. So after two further hours of sailing, even these giants were mere specks on the horizon. But he kept the full crew on deck throughout the night just to be on the safe side. By first light, the harbour entrance of his peninsula destination was clearly in sight. Two more hours saw him alongside a smelly Indian Ocean *jahazi*, furiously arguing to be allowed to dock. He pleaded that he had urgent news for the Harbour Master and that he must cross their ship to get ashore.

Paying a few silver pieces to convince his would-be host, he was soon ashore and heading for the Harbour Master's office. Ahmed remained on board to tend the *Tajir* and its cargo, a mixed offering of textiles from Gujarat and Coromandel in India and tin from western Malaya ports further north, which he would carry westward on his return journey. But the trading would have to wait. For now, his most important mission was to warn the local garrison, meagre though it was, of the presence of the strange intruders into their realm.

"Nonsense," said the Harbour Master. 'No ship on the Ocean Sea is that big. What have you been smoking?"

"As Allah is my witness," protested Ohmar, "I saw it with my own eyes not two days ago. And not just one either. I saw at least four of them. And they were accompanied by dozens of other strange-looking vessels, all of different sizes but all bigger than my ship. I tell you, there was a whole fleet of them."

"In your dreams, maybe," said the Harbour Master, his patience clearly wearing thin with this ridiculous sea clown. "Be off with you before I call the guard. I have better things to do than listen to your nonsense."

Ohmar could see that he wasn't going to get far with this conversation, so he quietly and subtly bowed and made his exit. He did not see what more he could do. He had tried to warn the authorities of the potential danger, and they had dismissed him as a fool. His conscience was clear. It was time to start his trading, the business that he was here to do.

This was his first voyage to the far east of the Indian Ocean. But he had been aware of its exotic offerings from the many conversations he'd carried on along the northern coastline of the great ocean over several decades. Most ports had a spice market and a gold souk. Most had a timber market too. Ohmar had visited most on each of his port visits, searching for trading opportunities along the ten thousand kilometre coastline, from the head of the Persian Gulf to the Malay Peninsula, around the protrusion of the Indian sub-continent into that vast water world. There were hundreds of ports, both large and small, along that seafaring path, including the important trading ports of Basra, Bandar Abbas, Mumbai, Kollam, Kolikata, Dhaka, Dagon, Bharukachchha, Champa, Chaul and Satgaon. Some were now fading, but each offered its own unique trading opportunities. Each was hungry for the wares of the others, and Ohmar's family had earned a lucrative living for generations carrying and trading with them. But these markets were always on the lookout for something new. The novelty of these new offerings made them super-profitable, which was, of course, the key to becoming really wealthy.

Ohmar was not sure what exotic offerings might be available this far east. But he was confident there would be something. In particular, from what he already knew, he sought nutmeg, mace, and cloves from the Moluccas, gold and pepper from Sumatra; camphor from a distant land called Borneo, and sandalwood from an even more distant one called Timor. And from the Malay Peninsula itself, he already knew and had bought tin and now sought more of that commodity. All of these, he already knew, would sell most profitably in the Indian, Arabian and African ports from whence he'd come.

But what else might be available? Things that even he had never seen before and which would delight his more western customers and loosen their purse strings? At this time, he did not know, but he did know where to find out.

He headed straight for the main marketplace as soon as he quit the Harbour Master's office.

Ohmar was in the spice souk when the commotion broke out. He was sampling cloves with an amiable but cautious Malay merchant when the ambient conversation rose in pitch and audibility, particularly on the seaward side of the market. Customers started edging away from their negotiations and glancing anxiously toward the gathering throng crowding around the entrance to the small jetty that jutted into the bay.

At that point, Ahmed emerged from the crowd, his gaze darting left and right as he sought out his quarry. It finally settled on Ohmar and he rushed towards him.

"What's going on?" demanded Ohmar. "You're supposed to be with the ship."

"Yes, master," gasped Ahmed, "but you must come

quickly. They've followed us," he added breathlessly.

"Who?" asked Ohmar. "And what do you mean 'followed us'? Who's followed us?"

"The great ships," said Ahmed. "They've followed us. Well, at least one of them, anyway. It's anchoring in the bay right now."

Ohmar turned pale. He thought they had outrun them, got clean away, but now it seemed that all the *Tajir* had done was to lead them directly to Malacca. He'd already told the Harbour Master of their encounter with the strange fleet so there would be no doubt in official quarters who had brought this misfortune upon them.

Ahmed turned away and headed seaward, motioning Ohmar to follow him. The two pushed through the crowd until they were amongst its vanguard. Before them lay the great ship, now lowering its bamboo sails in unison from each of its nine masts. Off to her port lay a smaller vessel about half her size. This was also now swinging on its anchor cable. Behind her was a third vessel, somewhat larger than the smallest ship, but which Ohmar could not discern clearly as she was partly obscured by the greater one.

The great vessel was now beginning to pivot on the stretched anchor cable sloping away from its bow and down into the depths of the bay. The wind rotated the great hull to leeward, pointing its bow back out to sea and into the face of the south-westerly breeze. Along the length of the main deck, small rowing boats were being swung out of wooden divots and lowered into the calm waters in the ship's lee. Ohmar could see about six of them. A small group of men crowded around the lowering divots, some carrying spears, most carrying strangely curved swords. Most were dressed in a stiff brown covering that looked like leather.

"I don't see anything that looks like cannon, do you?" asked Ohmar to his anxious mate.

"No," said Ahmed. "And none of those men seem to be carrying any fire poles either."

"Perhaps they haven't got any," said Ohmar. "Maybe they haven't got that sort of weaponry," he speculated. "Let's hope so."

The seamanship of the visitors seemed crisp and efficient, and soon all six small commuter boats were pushing away from the side of the great ship. Each vessel appeared to have civilian as well as military personnel on board. Most of the former were dressed in blue or greenish robes with hats that resembled upside-down sewing baskets with a black crown and a red cherry on top. The exception was the central boat which carried a person dressed in a red robe with a black hat. Most robes looked quite plain, but the red robe bore gold adornments on its sleeves and collar, suggesting that this latter figure was the senior member of the shore party. The military types were dressed in a dull brownish tunic overlayed by outer leather vests, shoulder pads and pleated skirts, presumably a form of armoured protection.

The crowd watched curiously and with apprehension as the small fleet of boats approached the pier. Just as they were about to reach it, Ohmar felt a tug on his sleeve. He glanced sideways to its originator, a robust man wearing a metal breastplate and steel helmet and armed with scabbarded scimitar hanging from his belt.

"The Shah demands your immediate attendance at the palace," said the soldier.

"Me?" queried Ohmar. "Why me?"

"You are the ship's captain who reported sighting a strange fleet, aren't you?" demanded the guard.

"Why, yes," said Ohmar. "I am."

"Good," said the guard. "Let's go."

And with that, he grabbed Ohmar's arm and gave it a firm tug.

As Ohmar was led away, he shouted back to Ahmed, "Go back to the ship and stay with her. And don't let anyone on board." Then he was gone, leaving the bewildered Ahmed to his own devices. So back to the *Tajir* he went, boarded her, and drew up the gangplank.

Twenty minutes later, Ohmar was ushered somewhat roughly into the presence of the Shah. The Harbour Master was there with him, looking rather sheepish. A dozen or so other officials surrounded the local ruler, as well as the commander of the local garrison and a few of his subordinates.

"What can you tell me about this strange fleet that you saw out in the strait?" demanded the Shah.

Ohmar recounted what he had told the Harbour Master earlier that morning. The minor officials were now looking decidedly worried as Ohmar recounted how he had not been believed and told to "be off". The Shah waved the matter away.

"You say there were dozens of them?" he inquired. "How many?"

"I saw four of the size of the ship in the harbour, Excellency, but there may have been more. They were accompanied by about twenty other vessels but of smaller size but all at least twice the size of my ship, which is twenty-eight arash (about sixty feet)."

"So these three ships are just a small part of a much larger fleet, are they? What course did they appear to be making?"

"North, Excellency, as though making up the strait. Quite

frankly, we thought they had not seen us. We veered away shortly after seeing them and headed straight here. We didn't think any of them had changed course to follow. Otherwise, we would not have come directly to this port. We would have led them somewhere else."

"Yes, yes," interceded the Shah impatiently. He was used to people making excuses to try and stay out of trouble. "Is there anything else of importance that you can tell us about these ships?"

"I don't think so, Excellency. I've told you all I know."

"Alright," said the Shah. "Dismissed," he added curtly.

Then he turned to the captain of his guard. "It looks like they're sending some sort of delegation," he said. "You'd better get down to the wharf and greet them and invite their leaders to join me here for refreshments.

"Take about twenty men with you and leave half of them at the pier to watch the boats. Full armament and weaponry, but be diplomatic. Don't let anyone go anywhere until I've had a chance to talk to these strangers. We don't want them spying on our defences until we know what they're doing here."

Just as Ohmar was about to meekly take his leave and unobtrusively head back to the pier, a small commotion developed at the entrance to the large reception hall of the Malacca Shah's palace. Through its double doors marched the captain of the port guard, followed a few steps behind by a round oriental man in flowing red robes and an elegant black circular hat of upturned conical shape crowned with a black velvet top and adorned with a bright red cherry. One step behind and to his right followed a similarly dressed man in a deep blue robe, and to his left, one step back was another similarly dressed man in a greenish robe.

Following the two wingmen in single file were three military types in brownish tunics with brown leather overlays. Each wore an ever-widening tapered sword which suddenly scooped back to a sharpened point from the three-quarters length downwards; the swords hung menacingly from thick leather belts. The whole party was flanked by five of the shah's guardsmen on either side, each brandishing a multi-pointed halberd and wearing a scabbarded sword on his belt.

The captain marched up to within two paces of the Shah, bowed low and said:

"Excellency, I present to you Ambassador Chin Lui Chow of the court of the Emperor of China and envoy of Admiral Zheng He, commander of the Great Fleet of which his ship is part." He then backed off and moved to his right, leaving the way clear for the exotic visitor to move forward to where he'd been standing.

The Ambassador took two paces forward, paused and looked the Shah directly in the eye. Then bowed low from the waist, paused momentarily, then straightened without waiting to be invited to. He said in a firm tone voice, with an almost haughty tone, in broken Malay:

"Greetings, Excellency. I bring you the warm felicitations from the Lord of Heaven, Emperor of the Middle Kingdom and Master of the World, the Mighty Zhu Di and his loyal servant, and my master, Admiral Zheng He."

"You are welcome," intoned the Shah, somewhat taken aback by the arrogance of his guest. Nevertheless, he was determined to at least maintain as peaceful a discourse as possible, given the size of his visitor's vessel and the meagreness of his own garrison. "To what do we owed the pleasure of this meeting?"

"In a word, Excellency, trade," replied the Ambassador.

"China has everything that it needs, but the Mighty Zhu Di is mindful that not all are so fortunate. He desires to share his abundances with others elsewhere in the world. But he would not insult them by offering them charity, so he seeks to trade anything that might be of use to the Chinese people in exchange for his sharing our wealth and culture with them."

"That is most generous of the Emperor," said the Shah. "What is it that you have to offer us?"

"I can best answer that by showing you," said the Ambassador. "If you would care to join us on board my ship, I can show you what we have to offer."

"Perhaps you could unload a small portion of your wares on the pier, or even set up a stall in the market-place to display what you have to offer," said the Shah. "That way, our merchants can gather around to view your samples, and you could view theirs."

"An excellent suggestion, Excellency," responded the Ambassador.

"In the meantime, Ambassador, would you and your party care to join us for some refreshments? It will give you an opportunity to enlighten us further as to the wonders of your homeland."

"You are most kind," said the Ambassador. And so they did.

The great ship offered an exotic cargo of silk and porcelain from China in abundant quantities, a small portion of which its crew unloaded overnight in a prominent place at the entrance to the market-place. As a guest at the initial refreshment invitation, Ohmar was also invited to accompany the Shah and his entourage on an inspection tour of the ship later that afternoon. He was also first in line to tour the display pavilion set up by the visiting traders the next morning. It proved to be the start of a long trading relationship.

806 AH was the date of Ohmar's first encounter with the great fleet (1404 AD by the Gregorian calendar). For the next thirty-two years, Ohmar plied the trade from Basra to Malacca and back again. The great fleet did not return every year, nor did it always stop in Malacca. From the very start, it travelled much further around the coast to India. It even sailed southward down the African coast as far south as the Swahili coast on one occasion.

Ohmar grew rich on the trade. Then in 836AH (1433 A.D.) the voyages of the Great Fleets from China stopped, never to sail again, and Ohmar had no idea why.

Oecussi Caravel – 1512 A.D.

The *Explorador's* deck leaned ten degrees to leeward as the south-easterly breeze caught the vessel's lateen mainsail and mizzen sail as she cleared to the headland. Her pace quickened to just under ten knots, while her rudder steered to port to begin her trip along the north coast of Timor on the start of her 2,500 leagues (fourteen thousand kilometres) trip back to Lisbon from whence she'd come. Her foremast still held the square-rigged sail that had powered her northward out of Lifau. But its three-quarter reach now swung more or less into a downwind run, billowing square on to the following breeze as she swung to the west on a journey along the coast, across the Sulu Sea, on past the Komodo Island with its fearsome dragons, and the along the north coasts of West Nusa Tenggarra and Lombok. Then she would cross the Lombok Strait, skirt the north coast of Bali, cross the sea that bears that island's name and on to the north coast of Java to the port of Surabaya. There, she would complete her manifest with whatever opportunistic, high-value cargoes were available to fill the minimal space remaining in her hold.

She would then head west again along the north Java coast to the Sultanate of Demak. There they would pick up a navigator who had reputedly sailed straight across the Indian Ocean five times to Mozambique and its Portuguese trading post that the *Explorador* had visited on its outbound voyage.

The diagonal cut across the great ocean would cut hundreds of leagues (thousands of kilometres) off of the homeward leg than if they hugged the coast like on their outbound voyage when they had steered up the East African coast, across the Arabian Sea, around the Indian Sub-Continent, across the Bay of Bengal and down the western coast of Malay Peninsula. It would be an epic sea crossing and an important contribution to Portuguese seafaring knowledge of the Far East that no European had done before. Malays had been doing it for centuries, but this whole venture was new to Occidentals.

The outbound course had been necessary, given the pioneering nature of the venture. *Explorador*, despite her name, was not an exploration vessel. She was a trader, her prime objective to profitably trade, preferably in high-value goods. She had left Lisbon one August day in 1511 after the fleet led by Admiral Afonso de Albuquerque, in the service of King Manuel I of Portugal, had orders to seize control of the spice trade from the Arab traders who had dominated it since the Roman Empire. Alfonso had done his master's bidding and seized the port city of Malacca later that year, which then was the hub of Asian trade.

In November that year, having secured that central hub and learning of the location of the Banda Islands – home of that most lucrative commodity, nutmeg – Albuquerque had sent an expedition of three ships, led by his friend António de Abreu, to find it and secure it. *Explorador* had simply followed in Abreu's wake all the way to Oecussi.

The Admiral's faithful lieutenant still had nearly two hundred leagues (over a thousand kilometres) further east to travel to reach the fabled islands but, from a commercial point of view, the commodities available in Oecussi, and the various ports of call along the way, had already filled the *Explorador*'s hold to almost overflowing. Since the first ship home was bound to reap the greatest of rewards, *Explorador* had elected to head home now and beat the rush of the homecoming Albuquerque fleet and its bountiful loads.

That was entirely appropriate given the caravel was not in the King's service, was under no royal orders and was a purely commercial venture. Her owner was not the King of Portugal – it was a consortium of Portuguese businessmen led by the Guardian of the Duque de Beja, the King's infant nephew. Although not of royal blood, he was sufficiently close to the House of Aviz to know most of the King's secrets even though he was not formally part of the King's court.

The wily noble was an astute businessman. Not only did he plan to steal the march on the King's exploratory fleet, he had also ensured that a young officer, loyal to him, was among the crew of each of Albuquerque's ships. These spies could enlighten him about what further opportunities might lay in wait further east when the main exploration fleet reached Portugal again. Assuming it did, of course.

As a final safeguard, he had appointed Pedro de Mascarenhas on the recommendation of Dom Garcia de Noronha, a leading investor in the venture, and also sponsor of António de Abreu, one of Alfonso captains now en route to Banda, as the new master of the *Explorador.* So if de Abreu's flotilla did not return, then the *Explorador*'s cargo would be the most lucrative prize if it alone returned. If not, it would be so by its being the first to return. Pedro's main objective now was just to get the *Explorador* home safely.

It had been a good trade. The last of the metal manufactures from the Iberian Peninsula had raised much interest and sold for good prices in the Lifau marketplace as they had done in previous ports of call since leaving the Cape of Good Hope. The Indian rice and fine textiles picked up along the way had also sold well. There had also been substantial interest in the gold and silver coins amongst local traders, though more out of curiosity than anything else – the locals weren't sure of their trade value, having not seen their like before, but nevertheless appreciating the intrinsic value of the precious metal content. So, all things considered, the *Explorador*'s trade offering had been well received in the small community that populated the small port and its hinterland, sufficiently so that the seventeen-metre long caravel was now fully laden with one of the most precious cargoes on earth: three tons of nutmeg, mace and cinnamon, two tons of deer horn, half a ton of bees wax and fifty-two tons of sandalwood.

But nothing was certain. The Lord of Demak had been friendly on the outbound leg of the eastward journey, but that did not necessarily mean he still was. Afonso had made peaceful overtures to him after he'd taken Malacca, but things were still in a state of flux. The Demak lord had only recently become Sultan, given his ancestral lineage to the hereditary rulers of the great Majapahit Empire, which had dominated the north Javanese coast and the Malacca Strait for several centuries. But that empire was now fading. The fierce staunchly Islamic Sultan of Tenate was flexing his muscles in the region and his Arab dhows could appear on the scene unexpectedly at any time.

The Sultan had welcomed the Portuguese mercenary contribution to help in his struggle against his rival, the ruler of Tidore, earlier that year, but he'd barely hidden his disdain for the Europeans. His ships were every bit as fast as the *Explorador*, even if the caravel could easily outrun the great, lumbering Javanese Jong behemoths which were four times the size of the Portuguese vessels, and could carry military forces far superior to his own and needed for close-quarter fighting.

Nor could Pedro rely on his superior seamanship to save his ship, his crew and his cargo if challenged. The Javanese, and their Sumatran neighbours, had been plying these waters since the great Srivijaya Empire a thousand years earlier, and had long mastered the trans-Indian Ocean trade Pedro hoped to exploit for his own advantage. That ancient North Sumatran seaport had grown rich by extracting tribute from any vessels sailing the Malacca Strait. That long tradition was still alive and well, with privateering locals still operating in regional waters long after the birthplace of legally-sanctioned piracy had slipped into distant memory.

Luckily the *Explorador* had one advantage the locals did not have – she carried six swivel cannons, two on her bow, two on her after quarters and one on each side of the forward corners of her stern castle. All Afonso's fleet was so armed, which had given him the crucial edge in his conquests in the Far East to date. Also, the *Explorador*'s crew had muskets and knew how to use them. The caravel was not a warship, but she was far from defenceless.

But Pedro hoped he would not have to use any of this firepower – it was better to skirt trouble if possible as even the most apparently favourable of battle conditions could turn sour in a moment – most military engagements usually resulted in some casualties and some damage. He could ill afford either being so far from home, in unfamiliar waters and with unpredictable and unreliable allies, if allies they even were.

Nor was the risk of piracy in the Indian Ocean proper insignificant either. The taking by force of the ships and cargoes of others, usually accompanied by the despatch of their crews in cold-blooded fashion, had long been a tradition in this ocean. The discovery of the route to "the Indies" by Vasco da Gama in 1497 had only amplified the phenomenon and added a new European flavour to the practice. Da Gama himself had committed some fairly barbarous acts during his expedition, including acts of piracy against unarmed Arab merchant ships and the firing of his cannons on the cities of Mozambique. Portuguese ships were as feared and as unwelcome along the coasts of East Africa as much as any would-be cut-throats, so the *Explorador* was unlikely to meet with a sympathetic welcome from anyone who had been on the receiving end of the exploits of her European forebears or contemporaries.

No matter what the hazards, however, the trans-ocean voyage was the quickest way home, so that was the path *Explorador* had to take. There was no other alternative if she was to get home first. What lay along that path, however, Pedro had no idea. Abyasa, the Javanese navigator Pedro had taken on board in Demak, had said there were islands en route about halfway across the ocean. But he was no more informative than that. There was rumour of a great land to the south-east of Java, but no-one seemed to know anything specific about it, so Pedro could not even be sure it existed. His chart showed the detailed coastlines of the East African continent and the eastern shore of the Madagascar Channel, with some roughly sketched outlines of the Southern Sumatra coastline he had taken from Javanese maps. Beyond that, his chart showed a huge blank space all the way from the Sunda Strait to Dar-es-Salaam.

There had been rumours amongst some Arab traders that their brethren had traded with some islands somewhere in the western regions of the ocean, east of the Madagascar landmass. But no one seemed to be sure how big that great island was or how populous those fabled islands were, except for, or unless the reference was to, Mauritius, which had been charted by Portuguese navigators in 1507. And this was known to be relatively modest in its trade potential. Pedro indeed was sailing into the unknown.

Explorador cleared the Sunda Strait without incident and set out on a west-south-westerly course directly for Dar-es-Salaam on the South-East African coast. From there, Pedro would be in waters for which he had reasonably reliable charts. But nine days into the journey, the bow lookout suddenly screamed:

"White water, white water dead ahead."

"What bearing?" demanded the watch officer.

"Everywhere," yelled back the clearly panicking seaman. "It's everywhere – right across the horizon."

"Heave to," yelled the watch officer. "Captain to the quarterdeck!"

Pedro briskly mounted the wooden gangway to the quarter-deck, extending his telescope as he cleared the uppermost step. "Report," he snapped.

"White water, sir," responded the watch officer. "All along the horizon to starboard as far as the eye can see."

Pedro squared off to steady himself to the rolling of the deck and raised his spyglass to his right eye. He scanned the horizon fully from north to south – no doubt about it. One continuous reef stretched as far away in both directions forming an apparently impenetrable barrier to the *Explorador*'s further westward passage.

"Get Adyasa up here," he snapped.

The clearly troubled Javanese mounted the gangway to the

afterdeck in response to his summons. He joined the captain next to the starboard guardrail.

"Well," snapped Pedro. "What am I looking at here?"

"I don't know," said Abyasa, his voice trembling.

"What do you mean, you don't know? You're supposed to know. That's why you're on this ship. Why haven't you told me before that I'm likely to encounter this?"

"I don't know," bleated the now terrified navigator. "I've never been this far south before."

"What do you mean," shouted the now enraged captain. "You said you had sailed these waters five times before. Are you telling me that you lied?"

"No, sir," pleaded the oriental. "I *have* sailed this ocean before, five times, just like I told you. But for three of those times, we encountered no land between Java and Africa, and on two occasions, we called in at an island group the locals called Maldives. But I think that we're well south of that here, by about a hundred leagues (around five hundred kilometres) by my reckoning. I've never been this far south before."

"Why didn't you tell me that before?" demanded Pedro. "Why didn't you tell me that you had no idea what lay before us?"

"I had nothing to report," wailed the hapless man. "I had nothing certain to go on. You have not permitted me to view the daily log, or your charts, nor sound the ship or even given me access to your sandglass, as *you* have recorded or plotted our progress. I have had to rely only on my own observations of our speed and the time of day. I'm only guessing where we are now. You have not kept me informed of our speed or progress since we last saw Sumatra."

Pedro turned a brilliant shade of red. "So you're saying that your incompetence is all my fault?" he challenged menacingly.

"Is that your excuse? You are supposed to be a navigator. You should not need my equipment to know our position if you have the skills you claim to have. Or have you lied about that too?"

"I'm just saying that, if you had taken me more into your confidence in my capacity as navigator, I could have been more precise in my advice. I could have been more certain about where we actually are, and I could have pointed out to you that these waters were beyond my personal experience."

The Javanese mariner had regained a little of his composure by now, and tried to sound as reasonable as possible in his current precarious position. But Pedro was not the type of man to allow a subordinate to transfer blame to him, no matter how justified such might be. He turned away from the navigator and barked a savage command:

"Master-at-arms to the quarter-deck, with firearms and the guard."

The master-at-arms quickly responded to his summons dressed in breastplate and steel helmet and carrying a pistol in his belt and a sword at his side. He was promptly followed by three similarly dressed, musket-carrying marines.

"Throw this fool over the side," he ordered. The quartet moved forward in unison to carry out the order. The order had been in Portuguese, but the Javanese man had by now learned enough of that language to instantly understand what was about to happen.

"Excellency," he pleaded. "I have only done my duty. I could not report to you without knowing what our true position was. Mercy, Excellency. Mercy".

Pedro turned on the terrified victim, his voice laced with venom and vindictiveness. "Do you realise that if the wind had been just one knot stronger, we would have arrived at this point in the middle of the night? We would have had no time for the lookouts to sight that reef. We would have run straight onto it, and it would have ripped out the ship's hull in an instant. Everyone on board would have died because of your incompetence. Consider this your trial. I am the presiding judge, as the law dictates. You are charged with criminal negligence. I find you guilty. You are sentenced to death." He turned to the hesitating Guard Commander, "Master," he barked. "Carry out the sentence."

"Yes, sir," responded the Master and indicated his three subordinates to comply. The hapless mariner was hoisted aloft by the four soldiers.

"Over the transom," barked the Captain and promptly over the hapless navigator went. The small crowd on the quarter-deck gathered at the stern guard rail and watched as the man's bobbing body drifted steadily into the ship's wake.

"That is all," said Pedro calmly to the Master. "Return to your duties." Then he turned sarcastically to the watch officer and muttered: "Damned Orientals. You can't trust any of them."

Explorador sailed due south for five leagues (about twenty kilometres) before the white water started to recede into the distance. Pedro ordered the carvel's course to starboard by forty-five degrees and continued on a south-westerly direction for a further two and a half leagues (about ten kilometres) before the white water once again began to recede into the distance. He swung the ship around to his original course of two-six-zero degrees, and headed once again on a direct route to Dar-es-Salaam. The white water reef slowly drifted out of sight. At no time had anyone on board sighted land or seen any familiar land-based birds.

Explorador arrived in Lisbon three months later to great fanfare and lavish reward to Pedro and his sponsors. The crew bonuses were generous too. The whole voyage was a great success. Nothing untoward was noted in the ship's log on the trans-navigation of the Great Indian Sea.

Flower Power – 1637 A.D.

Flowers! Men tend to think of them as a female thing. You know, what you give to a woman when you want to win her favour. And you say it with flowers when you have really made a mess of things and want to say 'sorry'.

But they are more than that, much more. Apart from being the lure that flora uses to ensure its perpetuation, they can also be used as symbols – symbols anyone can recognise when no one dares to speak. Like the Red Rose vs the White Rose – which side are you on? Can I trust you? Am I safe with you?

They can be symbols of hope too. Like the four-leaf clover, something mythical, something hopeful. And that's powerful too. What could be more important than hope?

We use flowers to brighten up our dull, drab lives, to bring colour and joy. Or to say goodbye to a lost loved one, not so joyful but cheering anyway, to soothe the hurt, to assuage the loss.

So, bring me flowers if you care.

But flowers can also lead to folly.

That's what happened to Hans van de Bijl who got caught up in the craziness of the Great Tulip Mania of 1637 and lost a small fortune like most other investors of the time. He took a reckless gamble hoping it would set him up for life but failed disastrously. Hans contemplated suicide but lacked the courage to follow it through, so he ended as he began, a frightened little man who now broods his rashness. But his wife stood by him, his son left him, and his daughter resolved that her only future was to marry well.

But I'm getting ahead of myself. Let's go back to the beginning of this sad tale.

Hans van de Bijl was a slightly built, somewhat effeminate but agile man, standing 148cm tall with light brown hair and grey-green eyes. The forty-seven-year-old Friesland dairy farmer lived a sober life. He rose at dawn, ate a balanced, wholesome breakfast, worked steadily throughout the farming day, ate a light, wholesome, non-meat lunch, a hearty cooked dinner after dark, read in the candlelight of an evening, and retired early.

Hans had a brooding personality. He felt confident in situations where deep thought and careful consideration were required and, above all, sought order and predictability in his life. He felt insecure and tended to panic when pressured, so he disliked loud, bullying and demanding macho-types – like the old former school bullies –who still teased and belittled him, somewhat more subtly in adulthood, whenever the opportunity presented. He warmed to flattering, quiet-spoken people – like Anton Geisler, his boyhood friend and neighbour – which made him somewhat gullible and even occasionally encouraged a reckless streak in him – like the current debacle I am about to recount.

Upright, dependable Hans feared being outcast, disgraced or rejected, particularly by the leaders of his local community Lutheran church, which he attended for Sunday services in an attempt to win their respect, approval and acceptance. He craved financial success too, and was terrified at the prospect of failure. Secretly, he felt inadequate but tried to hide it. He yearned to break out, to be daring, to triumph, to be admired, but his timidity forbade it, so his weekly attendances at the Saturday market where he sold the produce from his small rural dairy property featured cautious but honest trading, which earned him and his family, wife Astrid, son Gerritt and daughter, Lesette, a modest but respectable living, and a modest acceptance as a little man.

All that changed in the winter of 1636, when Anton told him about *windhandel*, the 'wind trade', so-called because nothing actually changed hands. It was at the church fete the week before Christmas. Anton had just come back from visiting his cousin in Amsterdam.

"It's all the rage in the market district," he explained to Hans. "You don't need any money. All you do is sign a contract to buy tulip bulbs in the spring, then you sell the contract just before you're due to take delivery. The way the prices have been rising so fast, the selling price of your contract is worth much more than you've contracted to pay for the tulip bulbs. And all you have to outlay is two and a half per cent of the contract price as 'wine money' … to get you into the trading tavern, up to a maximum of three guilders per contract. So to sign a one hundred guilder contract, you only have to pay three guilders. But prices have been going up much faster than that. They went up from 120 guilders to 160 guilders in just three weeks in December, so if you buy 160 guilders worth now, at that rate, a bulb could be worth 210 to 220 guilders by the end of January. For an outlay of three guilders, you could make between 50 and 60 guilders pure profit in only one month. That's a return of over a 1,000 per cent in one month or 12,000 per cent per annum. And you don't have to just settle for one contract. You can buy as many as you like, 10 contracts, 20 contracts, whatever you like. My cousin made over three hundred guilders doing it last season, between October and November, with just four contracts."

"But who buys these contracts?" queried Hans.

"Anyone," said Anton. "You don't need any special qualifications or introductions, or be a guild member or anything. All you have to do is turn up at the tavern where the contracts are being traded, pay the 'wine money' to get in, and you can trade to your heart's content."

"No, that's not what I mean," said Hans. "I mean, who would actually pay for such a contract when all they get is a piece of paper."

"It's not just a piece of paper," said Anton. "It's a legal contract. You can enforce it in a court of law. If someone enters into a contract to buy the tulip bulbs from you at that price, say 200 guilders, for example, they have to pay you that, by law."

"But I don't have any tulip bulbs to sell," protested Hans. "I don't grow tulips."

"That's the beauty of it," said Anton. "You don't have to. The farmer who grows the tulips has the bulbs. He's the first one who signs a contract to sell them. And he does that so he is guaranteed as to what price he is going to get when they're ready to sell."

"But why would he enter into such a contract," said Hans. "Why would he contract to sell a bulb for say 160 guilders when he could get 220 for it when it's ready to harvest? It doesn't make sense."

"It does to him," said Anton. "By entering into a contract, he knows for sure, when he plants the bulbs, exactly what he is going to get for it. He doesn't have to worry about whether the market price goes up or down. He is guaranteed his contract price. It takes the risk out of farming for him. He can sleep at night knowing he's going to make a profit no matter what."

"But what if the market goes down," asked Hans.

"He still gets his contract price," said Anton. "If the market goes down, it's the person who entered into the contract to buy the bulbs at the contract price that would lose. But that's not likely to happen the way the market has been going for the last few years. Fortune favours the bold, my friend. Are you in or not?"

"Are you going in?" asked Hans.

"You bet," said Anton. "I've taken out ten contracts. So, do you want in or not?"

"And all it's cost you is 30 odd guilders?" queried Hans.

"Yes," said Anton. "I got in at 175 guilders. The market rate is 183 today, but ten contracts would still only cost you thirty guilders even at that price. You would probably have to contract to sell for about 250 to leave a profit in the sale for the person you want to buy the contract from you in a month or so's time. If you don't leave a potential profit in for the next buyer, no-one will buy your contract before it becomes due, and you would have to pay the full contract price of 250 guilders per contract."

Hans pondered the transaction. "I'll have to ask Astrid," he said.

"There's no time for that," said Anton. "Things are moving too fast. In any case, you know what women are like. She's bound to say 'no' just because she doesn't understand how finance works. I'm afraid it's now or never, my friend. Are you in or not?"

Hans frowned. This was not him at all: he was always so

careful with money. But then, everyone was talking about this. And it was not often he was given the opportunity to get in on the ground floor to such a lucrative business venture. This could be the opportunity he'd always hoped for. And Anton was right, 'fortune favoured the bold'.

"Can I get more than ten contracts?" he asked.

"Of course," said Anton.

"Good," said Hans. "I'll take a hundred."

"Right," said Anton letting out a low whistle as he did so. "You'd better come with me to Haarlem next week."

The return trip from the van de Bijl farm, thirteen kilometres west of Leeuwarden to Haalem where the most active tulip bulb 'tavern' was located, and back, took nine days. This allowed only one day at the trading site.

It was an arduous trip featuring long hours of horse-back travel frequently interrupted by long spells of walking to rest the horses and uncomfortable nights on straw mattresses in poorly appointed inns along the way. But at the end of it, Hans proudly displayed his hundred signed contracts to Astrid and assured her that this daring venture would set them up for life.

"But where did you get the money?" she inquired incredulously. "We haven't got that sort of money, not unless you've been hiding something from me all these years."

"I borrowed it from the bank in Leeuwarden before I left," he said.

"How much?" she inquired.

"Three hundred and fifty guilders," he replied matter-of-factly.

"Oh, Hans," gasped Astrid. "That's more than we make in a year. How did you get them to lend you that much?"

"I had to sign a Bill of Sale over the farm," said Hans. "But don't worry … that will be discharged in a few months when I sell these contracts. Then we'll be rich. We won't ever need to worry about banks again, not as a borrower anyway. They will want to borrow money from us."

Astrid said nothing more on the subject, initially because she was too shocked that her husband would do such a thing without discussing it with her. Later she reasoned that what was done was done. All either of them could do was hope and pray that all would turn out well in the long run. And she did pray, diligently, fervently, every night.

Hans had never been involved in securities or commodities trading beyond selling his farm produce at the local market in Leeuwarden. He'd relied on Anton for his initial advice on the 'futures' contracts, but even his knowledge was limited. So they had met up with Anton's cousin, Hendrik, in Haarlem the day before the trading day 'college' to plan a strategy for their respective ventures because prices had risen considerably since Hendrik's last highly profitable trade.

By the time they entered the trading tavern, the much-prized *Bizarden* bulbs were exchanging hands for 237 guilders a bulb. The *Bizarden* was the most prized of tulip bulbs because it featured a very rare tulip flower with yellow or white streaks on a red, brown or purple background.

Given the trajectory of recent months' price rises since the beginning of November, the trio reckoned that its price should be near 280 guilders by the end of February. Acting on Hendrik's advice to ensure a potential profit was still available to any would-be buyer of the contracts before that time, the three resolved to strike a price for the purchase of *Bizarden* bulbs on 21st February 1637 at the best price they could negotiate up to 250 guilders per contract. They actually achieved an average price of 247.25 guilders, a spread of less than three guilders between the lowest and the highest strike price over Hans' one hundred contracts.

Hans was well pleased with himself when he announced to Astrid the outcome of their trading on his return to the farm. If the price of the prized bulbs did rise to the anticipated 280 guilder level by the end of January, he stood to make a total profit of somewhere around 3,000 guilders – near ten times their annual income – which would set them up for life. If things didn't go so well, he only had to make about three and a half guilders profit per contract to break even on the whole venture, including travel and accommodation costs. Hans felt he was on a sure-fire winner.

But even the best-laid plans sometimes go astray. And that's what happened to the **van de Bijl** family in the spring of 1637.

The sure-fire winning venture to which they had committed came unstuck in two significant and unexpected ways. The first was the return of the dreaded bubonic plague, the Black Death. It re-emerged in the Netherlands that year, and was particularly virulent in the city of Haarlem, the very city Hans van de Bijl had expected to find a willing buyer for his 'futures' contracts for *Bizarden* tulip bulbs. Fear of the disease all but paralysed the city, and people stayed away from public meetings in droves. This included the informal 'taverns' where the speculative tulip contracts were usually traded. Traders – buyers anyway – simply did not turn up. So there was no market, and there was little if any trading of 'futures' contracts. Hans had no money to complete the contract by buying the tulip bulbs at any price, let alone the price he had contracted to buy them. He looked like facing bankruptcy from enraged counterparties eager to unload their plants at exorbitant prices.

The second unforeseen event had a more benign impact on Hans and his family. However, it still left them financially stretched. The Government of the United Provinces had become alarmed at the rampant speculation in tulip bulbs and sought to pop the bubble that had developed in that commodity by reiterating and strengthening the ban on 'short selling', first set in 1610 and reiterated in 1630. 'Short selling', the selling of a commodity before you actually owned it, with the intention of buying it to cover the sale at a lower price later, when an expected price drop emerged. The new rule did not ban the practice outright but was framed to render all 'futures' contracts unenforceable in a court of law. This effectively changed the contract from that of a future legal obligation to merely an 'option', meaning that a contracted buyer did not have to honour the contract and buy the commodity, if it was not in his or her best interest to do so.

This suited Hans just fine because the market price of his prized *Bizarden* bulbs had plummeted from its peak of 257 guilders three weeks after he had entered into his contracts to just under 100 guilders by the time his contact fell due near the end of February.

Naturally, Hans repudiated his contract, as he was now entitled to do – no point in buying tulip bulbs for 247.25 guilders if he could only sell them, or on-sell his contract to buy them at that price, for only the current 97 guilders.

But this financial rescue came at price for the van de Bijls. By repudiating the contract, Hans now had no interest in tulip bulbs, real or financial. His contracts were just worthless pieces of paper. But he still owed the 350 guilders to the bank that he had borrowed to get into the venture in the first place, plus interest accruing daily on that debt. So he owed more than a year's farm income just to repay the bank debt, and he had nothing to show for it.

"You fool! You reckless, stupid fool," wailed Astrid. "Look what you have done to us with your crazy get-rich-quick schemes. We're ruined, absolutely ruined. How are we going to get out from under this huge mountain of debt?"

But get out from under it they did. Hans and Astrid van de Bijl repaid their debt to the bank, but it took the couple most of their lives to do so. And despite her fury and anguish, Astrid stood by her husband throughout this time, although Gerritt and Lesette left within a year of the debacle. The couple was shunned by the local church congregation, and Anton, having suffered a similar fate, disappeared soon after his farm was repossessed by the bank to repay his debts. The remainder of the van de Bijl family had a very sober experience from which to educate future generations of the family into financial propriety and the prudence of spending only what you earned, managing your money wisely and to definitely avoid trying to get rich quickly by embarking on reckless business ventures in fields where you have no understanding of the full suite of risks involved.

Jaded Dreams – 1847 A.D.

"Ware ship."

The order was issued as a clear and crisp command from Lieutenant James Holbain. It was immediately reiterated in a firmer and more emphatic tone from the officer of the watch, Sub-Lieutenant Robert Galloway. It was then issued in a mighty bellow from the Master's Mate, Bobby Canardle, a seaman of the old school who had first shipped out as a powder monkey in the Home Fleet in the closing days of the great war with the French tyrant Napoleon Bonaparte.

The order's response was also prompt as the deck crew scrambled to their positions at the halyards and sheet lines that held the mainsails, the gallants and the topsails of the three-masted ship. The sailing crew rushed too, to the rigging and spar lines that carried the sailing crew aloft and out to the extremities of the yardarms that carried the ship's square sails. These great sails were now in full billow from the trailing south-westerly, and that force needed to be tempered as the ship swung to a more northerly route for the run up the eastern coastline of the Malay Peninsula.

The trip out from Calcutta had been uneventful with the steady sou-wester of the India Ocean trade winds yielding a swift fifteen-knot reach across the Bay of Bengal to the Irrawaddy Delta, along the coast of the Gulf of Martaban and on up the Yangon River, to the great trading port of

Rangoon. The tack to the south-east down the west coast of the Kra Peninsula had been equally uneventful, giving a good profitable leg in the mid-Peninsula port of Malacca. The *Vibrant* had taken on fresh supplies and water there before heading south again down the Malacca Strait to the tip of the peninsula and the bustling entrepot of Singapore.

But this last-mentioned leg had not been uneventful. A day out of the old Portuguese fortress port in the Malacca sultanate, they had seen a dhow several miles to windward, shadowing the English trader. She had stayed just out of gunnery range, but there had been no mistaking her intentions. She was there to observe the *Vibrant*. Her cargo and her capabilities had no doubt been assessed by spotters back in Malacca, and her presence conveyed to the privateers who paid for their vigilance. These privateers, or at least their scouting party, would now be those on board the dhow. They would be assessing whether it was a fair risk for an interception further down the coast where the strait was at its narrowest and where a small fleet of Sumatran pirates could quickly be assembled to seize the ship and her cargo.

But the *Vibrant* was not the usual Dutch, Portuguese or French trader, which was usually smaller and more lightly armed. The *Vibrant* was an English trader, one of the great ships of the Pacific and Orient Line. It was staffed with British officers and seasoned British seamen, the kind that had beaten the French emperor and had won command of the seas for Victoria. She carried only the latest in naval equipment, expertise and skill. She also carried twenty-four long-range cannon and a full complement of Royal Marines. She was not only the largest and fastest ocean-going trading vessel in the Far East, she was a formidable weapons platform, armed and manned by expert fighters.

The dhow shadowed the *Vibrant* for two days, then disappeared into the dusk of the second night and did not reappear again. Neither did any of her sister ships that cruised these waters hungry for easy prey. The shore spotters might have thought she was a juicy prize, but the pirate admiral was a little more experienced than them in the art of naval conflict. He had no doubt met British merchantmen before and had learned that it was more profitable to leave them alone. Some prizes were just too costly to take. The cargoes of the P&O line tended to be more like those than the other easy pickings that passed through the Malacca Strait, one of the world's busiest sea lanes.

The cargo of the *Vibrant* would have been a rich prize, though, as she carried the usual out-bound stores for the Chinese trading ports at the mouths of the Pearl, Yangtze and Yellow Rivers – mainly supplies for the trading houses of the Shanghai European quarter, little luxuries that made life more bearable for the homesick Europeans perched on the edge of the great Chinese Empire – frivolous things like pianos, plate glass, European-styled furniture and Indian muslin. But that was not her richest cargo. That was more compact, more concentrated and infinitely more valuable. It was the stuff of dreams, blissful dreams, and the P&O's Chinese customers craved it desperately. It was opium, sap of the poppy pods, scraped from the vast waving fields of the Afghan and Burmese high country and packed tightly into a concentrated form ready for distribution to the Chinese middlemen – they would pay ten times more than its FOB price to make even more profit downstream in the opium dens of the coastal provinces and further inland.

The Chinese government, both the provincial governors and in the Imperial Court, disapproved, of course. But there was little they could do about it. Demand was strong and growing exponentially, and the English were keen to supply. They needed to. They had little else, save for silver and gold, to trade for the Chinese goods that were so eagerly sought in England and on the European continent. Tea, silk, jade, exotic timbers, porcelain and many more fine manufactures were keenly sought in the markets of the West, but the Europeans had little that the Chinese wanted in return. Trade with the Orient had been draining European treasuries for nearly two centuries now, and a counter-trade commodity was desperately needed. Cultivating Chinese dope addicts had created the demand for a European-sourced commodity to balance the trade. Since England had captured the Indian sub-continent, more by guile, stealth and treachery than by force of arms, access to the poppy fields had come under English control, and so the golden cash crop to fuel the China trade had been found.

The British East India Company, that bastion of English entrepreneurial fervor, had come to dominate trade on the sub-continent. And the grand British shipping lines had come to dominate the Oriental sea trade, guarded and protected by the Royal Navy. On land, the private armies of the great trading house had turned the Indian principalities into vassals one by one, up until the mutiny, and the British government had taken over.

But that was later, in 1857. The real breakthrough on the China trade had come in 1839 when the Chinese Imperial Court tried to stop the drug dealers and enforce their own control over the opium trade in the treaty ports and the coastal hinterland of the South and East China Seas. That's when the armed might of the great British trading houses had really shown its strength. The Chinese imperial forces had been soundly beaten by the private armies and navy of the great British joint-stock companies, and, with the so-called Treaty of Nanjing in 1942, the Chinese had effectively lost control of their own country.

Now, the *Vibrant* and dozens, if not hundreds, of her sister ships plied their trade in the intoxicating drug, largely without hindrance from the sovereign governments, the sultanates, the principalities and the sheikdoms that lined the waters of the south, south-eastern and eastern civilisations of the Orient. Britannia ruled the waves, and few, even the most daring and desperate pirate bands who had extracted tribute from the Arab, Indian, Javanese, Malay and Chinese sailors for centuries, sought to plunder the P&O ships.

The *Vibrant* swung easily in a sweeping arc as the stern of the vessel responded to her rudder, and the bow swung smoothly onto her new heading of 27° magnetic.

"Steer full and by," barked Holbain. The order was repeated with firmness and volume by Galloway and even louder and more forcefully by Canardle. The sheet hands eased the windward sheets and pulled in the lee ones. The sailing crew adjusted the stay sheets and halyards to trim the sails to capture the stiffening breeze now flowing over the port quarter. The booms of the main and mizzen sails settled into the lee, and the sheet hands pulled their respective sheets and cleated them to secure the set. Forward the jib and flying jib sheet hands did likewise. The ship healed over fifteen degrees to leeward, and the ship settled into her new attitude and her new course.

"All set," reported Canardle.

"All set," reiterated Galloway.

"Very good," responded Holbain. "Carry on, Mr.

Galloway. You have the ship."

"Aye, sir," quipped Galloway in response. "I have the ship."

The *Vibrant* made Shanghai seven days later. There were no further incidents worthy of note on the run up the Malay coastline or along the southern Chinese coastline. They passed an outbound tea clipper four days out and paid her the usual maritime courtesies on passing. They also passed an American whaler that seemed to be riding high in the water, which suggested she had not yet found any sizeable quarry to fill her barrels ready for the homeward voyage to New England or the American west coast ports. They passed numerous Chinese junks of various sizes but saw no need to hail or acknowledge them in any way.

The Harbor Master's cutter drew alongside as the *Vibrant* cruised into Shanghai. She carried the general news reports from the Governor's information office, as well as the berthing details for the ship. She also carried a messenger clad in a royal marine uniform bearing a marine captain insignia and carrying a small brown leather satchel and a request for an immediate audience with the captain and the marine officer in command onboard the *Vibrant*.

It seemed there had been some further agitation amongst a new radical group of Chinese dissidents over the inequities of the current treaty arrangements with the foreign trading houses. No-one, it seemed, was quite sure who was behind the unrest. Many believed it had been encouraged clandestinely by the Emperor's brother. This was vehemently denied by official sources at the Imperial Court. Others said it was the work of a radical student movement, although no-one seemed to be able to specify who the ring leaders were. Either way, it seemed to spell trouble for the foreign trading companies operating from the treaty ports. P&O was alerting all of its incoming ships' masters and instructing them to provision promptly upon reaching port in case a hasty departure became wise and expedient.

Holbain thanked the marine captain for his briefing and the Harbor Master's officer for his advice. Then he called Galloway to his cabin.

"Cancel all shore leave, Mr. Galloway," he said. "Provision the ship as soon as we dock. Draw up the manifests for my signature, drawing from the company's warehouses as much as possible. Then just wait till I return from the company office before releasing any of the ship's company from duty. Also, ask our consignees to draw up their bills for acceptance but don't release the cargo until I return. Is that clear?"

Galloway paraphrased his captain's orders back to him, followed by a crisp "Aye, sir."

"That is all, Mr. Galloway," said Holbain. "Dismissed."

Galloway issued a further crisp, "Aye, sir," and exited the cabin.

Holbain turned back to the chart on his plotting table; studied it intently.

"What now?" he wondered. He had no idea where his next cargo was coming from, and he had no idea what his next destination would be. No doubt the company office would enlighten him further when he reached it later that afternoon.

Holbain did not know that in these early summer months of 1850, the China trade would be disrupted for the next fourteen years. A Chinese clerk named Hong Xiuquan, who had tried to advance his family's status by the time-honored tradition of passing the Imperial examinations and failed, saw God and Jesus in a stress-induced vision and became convinced that he was Jesus' brother. Millions flocked to his banner. By 1854, he had seized control of vast swathes of eastern and southern China, setting up his court in the "Heavenly Capital" in Nanjing.

At first, the British and other European powers did not quite know what to make of this new self-proclaimed divinity. They finally concluded that he was insane and threw their lot in with the embattled Qing regime of the old imperial court. It took until 1864 before the Chinese General Zeng Guofan could bring the rebels to heel and dispatch the mad pretender.

But this little saga was only just beginning as Lieutenant Holbain saluted the quarter-deck of the *Vibrant* and strode down the gangway to the waiting carriage that would take him to the company office to receive his new instructions. In any case, Holbain was not interested in Gods, causes or the dignity of the Chinese emperor. His bonuses were based on the profits that the ships under his command could make from the traditionally lucrative China trade. All he needed to know was what cargo was bound for what port and, most importantly, how much profit it would yield both to the great house that he served and to him personally. Jade and porcelain had been his two most lucrative Chinese exports in the last several trips, but would these commodities still be available with much of the interior in a state of turmoil? And if the charismatic visionary did prevail in his rebellion against the Qing dynasty, would he place the same emphasis on trade with westerners, reluctant and disgruntled though it had been in recent years? Or would he emulate his self-proclaimed brother and cast the traders out of the temple?

Holbain hoped not. That would not be good for business at all.

Holbain never reached the company office that day. Nor

was he ever to see it again. An angry crowd had blocked the path of his carriage not two squalid blocks from the wharf at which the *Vibrant* was tied up. He was forced to make a hasty retreat ducking missiles of fruit, vegetables and the odd firmer projectile as he did so. The *Vibrant* departed Shanghai an hour and a half later, her holds still almost full and her return to Calcutta profitless. She managed to pick up a small cargo of rubber at Kuala Terengganu halfway down the Malay Peninsula, but that barely covered the provisioning costs of the return voyage.

Thereafter, Holbain confined his venturing to Indian and Persian Gulf ports. They were much less troublesome. Until 1857, that is, when the sub-continent went up in flames. By then, he'd had enough of seafaring. By then he was ready for a quiet cottage in Devon. It was tranquil, greener, and boasted a much more congenial and neighborly company, even if it was a little cooler than he'd been used to in his restless years … and a lot less worrisome too now his financial fate was bound more to the fortunes of British Guilts than to the fluctuating fortunes of the P&O line.

Clotilda -1860 A.D.

Mather nodded sympathetically. "You're not the first plantation owner I've heard say that in recent years," he said. "The price of slaves is ruinous at the local slave markets. It's not much better further along the gulf and even around the Cape, *and* on up along the Atlantic coast. It's the damn Yankees and their abolitionist agitators. They have no sense of what it costs to produce cotton. But they're happy to take the profits when they ship it to England. They don't complain then."

"They have plenty of slaves in Brazil," said Hinton. "If we could get some from there and bring them in on the quiet, I know lots of owners who would be willing to take some – good profits available for any enterprising ship owner who wasn't too squeamish about what cargo he carried."

"Slaves aren't cheap in Brazil either," said Mather. "Better to get them directly from Africa."

"I doubt you'll get anyone to take that on," said Hinton, "not since the Smith trial in '54. He was lucky to get off with the judge ruling a 'mistrial'. Evidently, he was a foreigner and not an American citizen, or something like that. But the Yankees tried to nail him anyway. It's pretty well scared everyone off since then."

"It wouldn't scare me," said Mather. "And I've got the ships and the captains to do it too. All I'd need is a reliable buyer – one that I know would pay upon delivery. I couldn't go to court and sue him if he didn't so I would need to have a lot of confidence in his integrity. Plus, of course," he added pointedly, "a sizable up-front deposit to add an incentive for him to follow through on the deal."

"What sort of numbers are we talking about here?" queried Hinton.

"Oh, I don't know. One hundred and twenty-odd slaves selling for about, let's say, three hundred dollars apiece. Payment wise: a quarter upfront, balance on delivery."

"What sort of turnaround are we talking here, from down-payment to final delivery?"

"Well, a round trip to Africa and back, dodging a few British gunboats along the way, say six months – make it eight for contingencies. There's always a war going on in West Africa somewhere along that coast with slaves being part of the booty scooped up by conquering kings. Some they sacrifice in their religious rituals, but most of them they sell in local slave markets. The British have closed a lot of those down since they outlawed the slave trade in 1807, but there are still some operating in some of the stronger kingdoms, those that win local wars especially. It should be pretty easy to find out who's winning. Slave trading has been a custom there for centuries. It shouldn't be hard to buy slaves in their local markets and, given the abundance of supply, they should be cheap – cheap enough to make it profitable for everyone," reasoned Mather.

"Like where?" queried Hinton.

"Sir, you wouldn't expect me give away a valuable trade secret like that, would you? I mean, the value I add to commerce is not just the owning and chartering of ships … knowing where to sail those ships is a key service I offer."

"Quite so, quite so," said Hinton. "Your pardon, sir," pleaded Hinton with feinted courtesy. "Somewhat remiss of me to be so tactless," he added in his broad southern drawl.

"So," said Mather, "is such a proposition of interest to you?"

"Could be, could be," mused Hinton. "Can you leave me with that thought for a day or two? You'll be in Mobile for a few more days, won't you? Can we meet again on Thursday … how about lunch at my club; midday alright?"

"Fine, said Mather. "Until noon Thursday then. Good day to you, sir."

Thursday afternoon on 4th March 1860 saw Anthony Charles Mather depart from his luncheon meeting with Henry Albert Hinton with a banker's draft for 9,000 United States dollars drawn on a Mobile bank and payable to a Mobile goldsmith in his coat pocket. His brisk gait was accompanied by a firm square-set jaw and determined gaze. He headed in the direction of his shipyard office immediately adjacent to the main shipping wharf of Mobile harbour. Waiting there, as prearranged, was Captain Willis Arin Forrester, master of the schooner *Clotilda*. His ship was moored directly in front of the office, and its twelve-man crew was squared away for immediate departure. An hour later, with Forrester aboard and in full command, the ship slipped its moorings and headed seaward, its course due south until it cleared Dauphin Island. Then it sailed southeast, apparently heading for Havana in Cuba.

But *Clotilda* was not heading for the Spanish seaport. As Marquesas Keys at the most westerly point of the Florida Keys drifted lazily past her port beam, she turned sou'-east by east on a mid-strait course, past Little Ragged and Inagua Islands then swung even more easterly until she cleared the last of the Caribbean Islands. Once out into the Atlantic Ocean, she headed directly for Monrovia on the West African coast. At a brisk pace averaging around ten knots, she arrived late in the afternoon of the 26th March. Here, Forrester busied himself catching up with local contacts from whom he could glean updated information on regional geopolitics and the fate of dispossessed peoples along the Slave Coast. He needed to be discrete, so it took a few weeks of subtle sleuthing to get a clear picture of the lay of the land further east. But he finally got what he needed.

"Dahomey," he learned, "that's where the best prospects lay at this time. But watch for Royal Navy ships," his informants warned. "Three British frigates have passed through here in the last three months with orders to stop the slave trade. They're still patrolling out there somewhere in the Gulf of Guinea. They're fast and well-armed. You'll need to be nibble to outrun one of those if they latch onto you."

Clotilda weighed anchor on 5th May and crept cautiously eastward towards the port of Whydah on the Dahomey coast. She veered away whenever a sail was sighted even though she carried no contraband cargo that would excite any intercepting vessel. But her passage would be noted by any ship passing close by, so it was better to stay unrecognised if possible. She arrived in the Dahomey port on 15th May 1860, where Forrester anchored a mile and a half offshore and landed in the longboat.

In Whydah city, six miles inland, Forrester immediately set about seeking out trade prospects of the dubious kind. And within a few days, he found himself ushered into the presence of a royal personage, the ageing cousin and former, now-deposed, king of that ancient kingdom and his entourage of roughly fifty officials. With cautious and diplomatic dialogue,

Forrester outlined his mission to His Highness. To his surprise, the prince's response was abrupt and definitive:

"I cannot see any problem, "said Prince Omonuwa. "In Dahomey, we have been trading slaves for centuries. We are an independent kingdom and we can choose whatever laws, rules and customs we see fit. The fact that the British might disapprove of some of our ways is of no concern of ours. We do as we please."

"So you see no impediment to our doing business in such a trade?" queried Forrester.

"Of course not," asserted the prince.

"And you have such commodities in stock?" inquired the captain.

"I have many thousands," said Omonuwa. "Take your pick. My factor will accompany you and assist with your selection. When you have selected your cargo, come back to me, and we'll settle the price."

And with that, he motioned to the attending official standing at his right shoulder to facilitate the inspection and selection of the commodity sought and turned away to indicate that the audience was at an end.

Forrester accompanied the prince's attendant out of the audience hall, but his liaison with him was short-lived. The latter escorted the seafarer to the prince's principal slave factor, introduced him, briefly spoke to the nodding agent in a language Forester didn't understand and then promptly left. The factor motioned the seaman to follow him. They walked through a winding maze of palace back alleyways until they came upon a large compound secured by two large double gates, twice a man's height. They passed through a smaller door in the left-hand gate and into a large square open courtyard.

Around the edge of the courtyard, lean-to shade canopies hung, sheltering upwards of five or six hundred souls – the prince had boasted of thousands – perhaps he had more elsewhere. Most were lying down; some were sitting, their backs propped up against the perimeter walls, and one or two dozen were standing. They appeared to have been segregated by gender, with about two-thirds being male and the remaining third female. Most appeared to be in their late teens, their twenties or in their early thirties, and there seemed to be several dozen pre-pubescent children of both sexes. There appeared to be a decided lack of elderly people.

The assembled multitude featured various shades of dark skin tones ranging from mid-brown to deep black. Almost all had short-cropped, curly black hair. Both sexes were mostly naked. Their facial features appeared to be distinctly different from those of the local Dahomey people that comprised the bulk of the local population, including the prince and his retinue.

"Mostly Tarkbars," the factor explained in surprisingly good English. "The king's soldiers took them in a raid on Tamale a month ago."

They all appeared to be in good physical condition.

"Take your pick," the slave trader added. "One hundred and twenty-five, I believe, is what you require."

Forrester hesitated, somewhat surprised at the apparent ease of the transaction. Then he composed himself and motioned to his first mate and accompanying leading seamen to commence the selection. He wandered between each of them as they did so, nodding his approval or shaking his head in disapproval as his best judgement dictated. The whole selection process took less than an hour. They finally assembled seventy-six men, forty-four women – ten pregnant

– and five children aged between eight and twelve, two male and three female.

The men were then shackled, hands and feet, with sufficient length to the latter so a brisk walking pace could be sustained. They were also secured with a neck collar with a meter-long connecting chain between them. They were organized into four lines of fifteen individuals and one of sixteen. Thirty-four women were secured with just a neck collar, seventeen in each of two lines. The final grouping was comprised of the ten pregnant females and the five children, also with neck collars only, in no particular order.

Forrester instructed the mate: "You follow on behind with the children and pregnant women. They won't be able to keep up with the main group."

"Aye, sir," said the mate.

"Jones," he said to the schooner's leading seaman, "you take the lead – straight back to the ship – no delays. Just follow the factor here."

Forrester turned to the factor. "I'll need two of your men to lead the second and fourth files," he said.

The factor nodded and barked an order in his unusual African tongue and two large black men, each carrying an impressive curved blade in scabbard tucked in his cummerbund, moved to the head of the two columns mentioned.

"Morgan, Hains and Hogarth," said Forrester to the other able-seamen from the schooner," you lead the rest and go with the lead group."

The seamen nodded.

"I'll bring up the rear of the lead group," Forrester announced, swinging a long barrel musket across his left forearm as he did so. "Right, let's move," he ordered in a slightly higher tone so that there was no doubt that this was a firm marching order.

It took almost two hours to return to the beach and a further hour and a half for Forrester and his first line of slaves to reach the ship with the longboat and two hired craft of similar capacity loaded with half of the remainder of the main party. Forrester ordered the loading of the cargo to commence immediately. The three commuter craft returned to the beach as the schooner's crew commenced chaining the human cargo into the ship's hold. The crew had just bedded the third line of fifteen hapless individuals, two with men and one with women, when the three commuter craft returned with the remainder of the lead party, again two with men and one with women. In the lead boat, however, the ship's longboat carried a worried-looking Harbor Master who scurried up the gangplank of the *Clotilda* to breathlessly confront Forrester.

"You have to go," he blurted. "Leave immediately. A runner has just arrived from our westernmost coastal lookout. There is a British frigate approaching from the west. She was about ten miles away when they spotted her sailing at cruising speed. The runner outpaced her, but that ship would have been travelling almost as fast as he can run, so she's probably only about an hour away. If you're still here when she arrives, she may demand to board you and inspect your cargo. You must leave now."

"Prince Omonuwa assured us that the British held no authority here in Dahomey," protested Forrester.

"Prince Omonuwa is not the sovereign authority here, not anymore," said the attendant. "The king tolerates his slave trading, but he will not confront a British warship to protect the prince's private business interests. The king has been telling the British that he is discouraging the slave trade. He will not contradict himself to save you and your cargo. Go now."

"But my mate is still ashore with the remaining slaves," explained Forrester.

"You have no time," said the attendant. "You'll have to leave him. I'll arrange for him to sell his slaves, but he will have to make his own way home. That's the best I can do," said the attendant. "Go now, while you can – head east. If you leave now, you should be able to outrun her. She will not suspect you if she doesn't get too close to you. She is probably heading for Porto Nova, so turn south at nightfall and get well away from the coast as quickly as you can."

As if on cue, an excited voice bellowed from the stern of the ship: "Sail-ho! Off the port beam, about ten miles," called the quartermaster.

Forrester whipped around to the direction of the sighting, extracting the telescope from his cummerbund as he did so. He pulled it to its full extension and raised the glass to his right eye. A three-masted ship filled the centre of his view. He judged the distance called to be about right. He could see the logic of the attendant's argument and could not afford to take the risk of losing his entire cargo. He eyed the African man momentarily, then barked:

"Get the rest of those slaves on board and secure them to the deck. Secure the longboat. Make ready to weigh anchor." Then he turned to the Harbour Master:

"Excellency, if you will," he said, motioning to the gangway.

"Good luck," said the servant, briskly descending the gangplank into his waiting commuter craft and moving to the stern of the vessel to enable the unloading of its cargo as quickly as possible.

The shackled creatures were dragged, pushed and bullied up the gangplank, followed quickly by those in the remaining two boats. Once chained to the deck fixtures: masts, bollards, rails, whatever was available, the crew set about weighing anchor and hoisting sails.

"Just the main, the mizzen, main jib and flying jib," ordered the captain. "Make for ketch rig; strike the colours, and break out the Portuguese ensign. Head 135° magnetic as though on course for São Tomé. Maybe they'll fall for it," he added ruefully.

Luck was on his side. The English warship did not alter course in pursuit. She sailed up almost to the spot where *Clotilda* had been moored and dropped anchor. Perhaps she was on a diplomatic mission after all.

As night fell on that eventful day, *Clotilda* changed back to schooner rig and altered course to the south-west. At dawn, she altered course again to west-northwest by west picking up the great circle trade route's westerly flow. Her course was now directed toward home, and her pace quickened to a brisk ten knots. All the slaves had now been stowed into the racks below deck where they would ride out the remainder of their trans-Atlantic voyage in miserable conditions. But not quite as bad as usual. The loss of fifteen slaves through their quick departure freed up modest additional room for each unwilling passenger. This resulted in the fatality rate being down to just three men and one woman from privation and none from outright starvation since surplus meals were available to ensure better nutrition en route – a fortuitous circumstance even if not humanely planned for.

As *Clotilda* approached Mobile Bay fifty-five days later, Forrester ordered the square sail yards and the top foremast to be lowered to give the vessel the appearance of a coastal trader. He discretely anchored the schooner just in the lee of Point aux Pins in Grand Bay with the crew, minus one mate, in good health and high spirits and at least one hundred and four African slaves in marketable condition.

Forrester took the longboat rowed by four crew members around the point to Coden, where he purchased a horse from a local farmer and made his way overland along a dusty track to Mobile. There he sought out Mather to announce his arrival. The jubilant merchant wasted no time in informing Hinton who, in turn, quickly spread the word to his "investors".

Two days later, at dawn, a small army of eager buyers with their accompanying slave masters discretely gathered on the south-eastern extremity of the city and proceeded back to Point aux Pins.

By evening of the 12th July, 1960, the impromptu slave auction had been completed with an average price of $326. Only two of the slaves, a sickly male and fever-ridden female, remained, unsaleable at any price. The entourage of buyers and their handlers disappeared into the night, making their own separate routes back to their various plantations. Hinton took his cut of the proceeds and departed, also leaving Mather, Forrester and his crew, plus the two hapless unsold slaves in his wake.

"And now?" queried Forrester of his principal.

"Now," responded Mather, "that's it – successful venture. Dispose of the ship. It's becoming too dangerous to chance our luck a second time. The Yankees have stepped up their patrols of the Caribbean, and you've already chanced your luck with the British. Providence was with us this trip, but I doubt He will be so generous a second time. And I doubt that you'll ever get the stink out of the ship now she's been used as a slaver, so she's really of no further use to us."

And with that, he mounted his grey, turned eastward and galloped off into the night.

Forrester promptly set about paying off the crew. When all had received their due and signed with their mark to witness receipt, he issued a final order.

"Swash the deck with tar and oil," he said.

"And the remaining slaves?" inquired the leading hand.

"Dispose of them," said Forrester.

"Aye," said the seaman. He descended the ladder to the hold. There he dispatched the woman with a single upward thrust of his dirk through her gullet straight into her brain. She saw and felt nothing. The sickly male saw her fate and struggled to rise, but the seaman was quicker, and a single blow through the prostrate man's right eye dispatched him with equal speed and finality.

Forrester was the last man to leave the *Clotilda*. As he stepped into the longboat, he turned and threw a flaming torch onto her deck. The oil ignited immediately, and soon the tar joined in. The schooner blazed brilliantly as they rowed away and was still burning brightly as they reached the shore.

"The boat is yours," Forrester said to the crew as he dismounted the craft. "Jones and Haines know the way to Coden around the point if you want to leave her there, or you can row all the way back to Mobile and sell her there. The choice is yours."

Then he strode to the horse he had tethered to a tree on his return with the buyers, mounted and turned the steed in the direction from whence it had come. He dug in the spurs and the horse lurched forward.

In his wake, the crew leaned into caucus on their next course of action. In the bay behind them, the *Clotilda's* blaze was dampening, and the vessel healed to starboard and started taking on water. She was the last ship to carry slaves from Africa to the United States of America, and it would be more than a hundred years before her wreck was discovered.

The Best Laid Plans – 1899 A.D.

Physically tough, but with decreasing agility due to sixty-three years of age, the brown-haired, brown-eyed, 175 centimetre tall, medium-built Captain Gerhardt Holdemann usually listened carefully to his second officer and closest friend, Lieutenant Kurt Kroner. His forty-seven years at sea – thirty-four with Norddeutscher Lloyd and earlier with several minor German trans-global lines – and his twenty-nine years as a ship's captain – fifteen of them with Kroner as his number two – the sober, and ever-dependable sailor had learned much about life and the perils of the sea. It had made him mentally tough too. He felt confident in command because he made sure he was served by a reliable crew. He disliked laziness, untidiness, unpunctuality and particularly incompetence, so together they had weeded out the malingerers, the unreliable and the drunkards. They had melded an efficient group of seamen into an effective, efficient, and experienced twenty-seven-man team who had confidence in them both on the small Far East German trader, *Östlich Händler.*

"You know," Holdemann had said, "if they had taken this ancient piece of steam-driven junk and replaced it with an oil-fired furnace, we wouldn't be in this mess today."

"What do you mean?" said Kroner.

"We wouldn't be looking for a coaling station right now

and the boys wouldn't need to do all this shovelling in all this tropical heat," said Holdemann. "The fuel would just be squirted into the furnace. Most of this heat would be gone and this filthy mess of coal dust wouldn't cover everything in the ship either."

"Could you do that on an old tub like this?" queried Kroner.

"I don't see why not, said Holdemann. "This is 1899, not 1839. Petroleum-based ships have been around for quite a few years now. They have a much higher energy-to-mass ratio than coal has. It would be much quieter, much cleaner and ultimately more economical."

Kroner looked doubtful. He was not sure the company would do that, even if they could. It seemed to him it would be cheaper to scrap this old tub entirely and build a new ship. But, knowing the company as he did, he couldn't see them doing that, not until they had extracted the last measure of work out of this old steamer.

He turned to the Engineering Officer. "What do you think?" he inquired.

"It sounds reasonable to me," said the ageing mechanic. "I'm not that familiar with this new-fangled piece of technology, but most of the British Royal Navy fleet seems to be moving in that direction, and all of the newer merchant vessels are oil-fuelled these days." It was an interesting thought.

The three of them talked about it over their evening meal in the cramped ship's mess where Holdemann had ravenously tucked into his favourite meal – Hamburg sausages and sauerkraut – minus the Pilsener beer since they usually didn't drink alcohol at sea. But they all knew that it was all academic anyway. Under the Meier and Crüsemann family leadership, the shipping company spent nothing it didn't have to, and the Siemen's board, the key charterer of this voyage with its dedicated cargo of electric locomotive engines bound for its latest branch in Tsukuji, Japan, had always been more interested in shareholder dividends than crew comfort. In any case, the 'old tub' was currently steaming through the Bismarck Sea on the other side of the planet from the companies' headquarters in Bremen and Berlin so even if Norddeutscher had want to update its transport assets to a more profitable fuel source, there was no way it could do it from here. So the crew of the *Händler* would just have to put up with the heat, and the mess, and the strenuous shovelling.

And they would have to find a coaling station out here somewhere too. That was brought home to Holdemann's attention pointedly at four o'clock the next morning by the Duty Officer.

"It's getting very hot down here, sir. The stokers are getting close to exhaustion. And the coal reserves are getting very low too. She's burning up our last hopper at a frightening rate. If we keep up this rate of knots, we'll run out of coal before we make Manila. We're going to have to slow down or we'll end up with dead men and a becalmed ship."

"Can we make Manus and pick up some coal there?" asked Holdemann.

"Possibly, sir," said the young lieutenant. "If the Spanish navy will give us some and always assuming that it's still in Spanish hands, the Americans may have taken it by now. If they have, do we know how they will respond to a German ship steaming into their newly conquered domain? Do we actually have any refuelling arrangements with them?"

Holdemann pondered the matter for a moment. This is not what he had planned. He was not a timid man. He was not afraid of anything much, save for the sea, which he held in great respect, and pirates who invested in this sea as voraciously as any that he'd encountered anywhere in the Mediterranean or the Middle East. But he was approaching retirement and looked forward to settling down with Gertrude in a little cottage on the North Sea coast. And the rumours of corporate intrigues, ruthless cost-cutting and early retrenchments had been circulating furiously throughout the industry in the months before he'd left Germany on this, what was to be, his last voyage. So an added risk gnawed at his subconscious: would he actually receive the pension that he'd come to expect after all these years of loyal, dedicated service to NDL?

So at his second but last port of call, Colombo, he had done a little side deal on his own initiative. In exchange for a personal commission of fifteen per cent, which he planned to share with Kroner and the rest of the crew, they had taken on board just under a ton of opium which they dutifully delivered to Rabaul and had been paid in American dollars for the illicit consignment. The bonus for the crew had been generous, and his retirement was now looking much more secure. The trouble was that this private arrangement had created a 2,000 nautical mile detour from their allotted course from Colombo to Manila. And fuel for that detour had not been included in their authorised replenishment at Colombo. He had assumed that Rabaul would have sufficient to top up, but their customer had not obliged, arguing that it was not in their agreement to refuel the ship. Since they owned the coaling resource, any replenishment would have been on exorbitant terms, so Holdemann had declined their treacherous terms and resolve to seek supply elsewhere, but from where?

The salt-dried, sun-tanned sea-farer usually rose at dawn,

ate sparingly in the ship's galley, stood the morning watch, toured different parts of the ship daily and ignored weekends. He had also spent his life at sea as a loyal and dependable German Far-East merchantman captain. Now, with this rash, out-of-character act of desperation, he faced a desperate situation that could lead to his utter ruin. He was still pondering his response when the young officer screamed into the bridge voice tube:

"Hostile vessel on the starboard bow! Shots fired. Heiliger Siegfried! That was close! It passed just over the bow. Captain to the bridge!" the frantic youth added, "Captain to the bridge!"

Holdemann was slightly puffing as he entered the bridge.

"Report," he barked at the clearly agitated young Duty Officer.

"On the port bow, sir. It looks like a Spanish gunboat. She's just ordered us to 'heave to'."

"All stop," barked Holdemann, "Hard to port."

"Spaniard signalling, sir," reported the Duty Officer somewhat redundantly. Holdemann had already noticed the yellow and blue flag flying from the Spaniard's signalling mast, the universal signal for *"you shall stop your vessel instantly"*.

"He's going to board," said Holdemann irritably. "Lower the starboard ladder."

The Spanish vessel came alongside and a boarding team, comprised of a fresh-faced young naval officer, a sour-looking petty officer, and two gun-toting seamen clambered up the rope ladder to the deck of the now languishing steamer. They climbed the metal ladder to the bridge.

Holdemann had picked up a smattering of most European and Far Eastern languages in his many ports of call so he recognised the signal and the young Spanish midshipman seemed to have also had picked up some German along the way. Together they managed to engage in a broken conversion about the ship's identity, its last port of call, its destination and its cargo. The young man examined the ship's log.

"It says here that your route is to be via Singapore to Manila, no?" queried the young officer. "So, what are you doing here?"

"We picked up a cargo of opportunity in Colombo," said Holdemann, "for delivery to Rabaul. We're on our way to Manila now."

"What cargo was that?" queried the inquisitor.

"Coffee," lied Holdemann without elaboration.

The young man frowned. He didn't look convinced. He motioned to the Petty Officer to look at the log. The PO looked even more unconvinced. He muttered a single word in Spanish, which Holdemann immediately recognised from his many visits to waterfront bars as reference to bovine mature.

"You are under arrest," the young officer announced somewhat triumphantly. "Follow me to Guam and stay within one kilometre of me at all times. Petty Officer Valdez and Seamen Gomez will remain with you until we get there."

"I can't make more than eight knots," said Holdemann. "I'm low on coal."

"Muy bien," responded the young officer. And with that, he and the remaining seaman returned to the gunboat, which then drew slowly away from the freighter and took up position five hundred metres ahead of the steamer.

The trip to Guam was uneventful if not anxious for Holdemann. *Händler's* coal was almost exhausted when they finally steamed into Apra harbour. But the slow trip had allowed Holdemann, Kroner and the ageing engineer to refine their coffee story The rest of the crew was ordered to say nothing more than that they had picked up cargo in Colombo but were not aware of exactly what it comprised. It sounded credible enough to military men who were used to being told only what they needed to know to carry out their duties competently.

The Guam Governor was not unfriendly towards Holdemann and his officers, and he paid them the usual courtesies as was customary between European gentlemen in the Orient. But he was a cautious man and felt it prudent to check the *Händler's* credentials with a little deeper probing. As for the young midshipman, he no doubt wondered why a cargo of coffee would be worth a detour of the magnitude that the German had taken, especially when such a cargo had not been recorded in the ship's log. The only evidence of the transaction was a substantial amount of American currency contained in the safe in the captain's cabin.

So, while he entertained the *Händler's* officers at Government House, he instructed the navy's non-commissioned officers to ensure the *Händler's* crew were well-dined, wined, plied with rum and accompanied by a most agreeable bevy of the island's most attractive young ladies.

After all, German interests in the South Western Pacific did anticipate that Spain would come out on top of the present confrontation between that still powerful European colonial power that had been in this part of the world for the past three hundred years and the new upstart kid on the block, the United States of America. Germany itself was a rapidly emerging world power, and trade prospects between the two European colonial empires could be lucrative if handled correctly. Best not to upset anyone, just check things out discretely and diplomatically, and smooth over any feathers the brash young midshipman might have ruffled.

The Governor would not receive any response to his cable from Manila to Bremen for weeks, given he would have to wait until the small coastal trader that left for Manila shortly after the gunboat brought in its prisoner, and another returned from there, his closest friendly port. Even then his cable would need to go via Japan, Russia and the Baltic to Germany because, although a trans-pacific cable via Guam was in the offing in a few short years, it was still yet to be a reality at this time. Also, he would need some fairly convincing evidence to hold the German ship until his communications with Holdemann's superiors could confirm his credentials.

Holdemann was aware of that too. He was also well aware that his superiors would not confirm his credentials, not his reason for being in the Bismarck Sea, anyway. So he was diplomatic but firmly asserted his right to freedom of navigation through Spanish-claimed waters, and he strongly protested his arrest as a violation of his maritime rights under the common laws and customs of the seas, particularly as they related to non-belligerent, friendly nations. He was getting desperate and his temper was wearing thin.

Holdemann buttoned the tunic of his best dress uniform and prepared for another innate round of conversation with his Spanish hosts. This time he was due to dine with the garrison captain and his young lieutenant and their wives at the garrison officers' mess adjacent to Government House. The captain of the British freighter, anchored two kilometres from the *Händler,* and the skipper of an American whaler, moored at the replenishment wharf on the opposite side of the bay, had also been invited. He would have preferred to dine with the Governor again since the suave aristocrat had not yet sanctioned his departure and he wanted to press him for permission to do so. But, since he and his ship were prisoners, he would have to at least appear grateful that he was dining with the best the colony had to offer, rather than tasting its dregs in the guardhouse.

He was about to don his somewhat battered officer's cap when a loud boom echoed throughout the ship. Almost instantaneously, the bridge voice pipe whistle squealed. He grabbed the earpiece and speaker funnel and barked into it:

"Captain."

"Sir, there is a rather large warship entering the harbour from the east. That noise that you no doubt just heard was the sound of her main armament. Six- to eight-inch, I would guess. She looks like a cruiser. It appears to be a warning shot because the shots fell well beyond the town halfway up the mountain to the north-west."

"I'll be right up," responded Holdemann.

He reached the bridge in less than a minute.

"Over the starboard quarter, sir," said Kroner, who was also in his dress uniform and who had beaten him to the bridge even without being summoned by the coxswain. "She looks like an American cruiser. She's flying her battle ensign, so she means business."

Holdemann seized the binoculars from the small shelf adjacent to his command chair and hurried to the rear starboard corner of the bridge. He peered through them, noting the details of the invader's superstructure: two masts, single funnel; single twin eight-inch gunned turret forward; three single six-inch gunned turrets along her port side, similar, no doubt on her starboard side. Basic battleship grey was her predominant colouring but with dapple bluish camouflage blotches and false bow shading to break up her visual profile. A large Stars and Stripes ensign waved in the light breeze from her forward mast. Yes, definitely an American cruiser and definitely in battle dress.

"Cancel all shore leave," ordered Holdemann. "We'd better stay out of this. Just sit tight until whoever wins this comes to us."

They didn't have to wait long to determine who that would be.

"The Spanish ensign at Government House has just been dipped," reported the coxswain. "It looks like the Spaniards are throwing in the towel."

"Wise decision," muttered Holdemann. He had not yet formally inspected the defences of the colony, but his host had advised at dinner two nights ago at Government House that he commanded a garrison of fifty-four men. He had not said that it was armed with any heavy weapons but the speed of the garrison's surrender now confirmed it. Had there been any artillery secreted in the hills around the harbour, it would surely have commenced firing by now. But there were no loud booms from either of the belligerents after the initial two-gun salvo from the cruiser's big guns, so the message had been successfully conveyed by the intruder from the outset. Resistance would have been bloody and useless.

The officers changed back into sea dress and waited. Holdemann saw the American shore party approach the main wharf and quickly disembarked as soon as they had come alongside. Concurrently, he had also seen a second armed party lining up on the cruiser's foredeck. Both shore parties rapidly deployed in brisk military fashion, suggesting they were US marines, men trained for just such operations.

There was no fuss ashore from local authorities. The shore party moved quickly up the main thoroughfare directly towards Government House, one column on each side of the street and with a small command group following cautiously twenty yards behind the sheltered column on the right. They reach the mansion within minutes, and the command group disappeared inside. A smaller group emerged fifty minutes later and headed back to the cutter from the warship, this time accompanied by a naval officer wearing a Spanish naval uniform and another wearing the uniform of a Spanish soldier.

Later that afternoon, the second cutter finally pulled away from the side of the warship and headed for the merchant vessels anchored in Apra harbour, first to the British ship and then to the *Händler*. The young man who climbed to the top of the bridge ladder and entered the wheelhouse was dressed in olive green battledress with high brown calf-length boots, matching belt and pistol holster. He wore a low domed 'tin lid' common to US marines and soldiers in times of war.

"Lootenant Alston, USS Charleston," announced the young, single-bronze-barred, bearded officer. "You are the captain?" he inquired of Holdemann.

"Ja," responded Holdemann tersely.

"I have been ordered to inspect your ship and ship's log, sir," responded the marine courteously. "Can you tell me your cargo and your ultimate destination," he added.

"Electric Train locomotives. Tsukuji, Japan," replied Holdemann again somewhat tersely.

"A little out of your way?" inquired the young man.

"I was arrested by a Spanish warship last week," growled Holdemann. "Illegally," he added. "I was sailing in international waters, peacefully, *neutrally*." He had emphasised the last word deliberately. "I demand the immediate release of my ship."

"May I see your ship's log," inquired the young boarding party commander. "And perhaps you could ask one of your men to accompany my sergeant to inspect your cargo."

Holdemann glanced at Kroner and motioned him to accommodate the last request. Kroner motioned the marine sergeant to accompany him, and they exited the bridge. Holdemann motioned his officer to follow him. "This way," he said and turned abruptly and headed for the starboard bridge exit.

The young officer glanced over the ship's log, nodded thoughtfully and said:

"Your log says that your last port of call was Colombo," said the lieutenant. "The quickest way to Japan would have been through the Strait of Malacca and via the South China Sea. What were you doing this far east?"

"We heard about the trouble between you Americans and the Spanish. We were trying to avoid getting tangled up in them. But, as I said, the Spanish navy had a different idea. No doubt they suspected that we were spying for the United States."

The young man nodded thoughtfully. "Thank you, sir," he said. "I'll report back to my captain and convey your request for a port clearance." Then he returned to the rope ladder at the side of the *Händler* and waited for his sergeant to join him. The two conversed for a minute or two, then demounted the ladder into the cutter, which then sped away from the German freighter and headed directly toward the American cruiser.

At dawn the next morning, as the *Händler* slipped unobtrusively out of Apra harbour, her coal hopper now full, courtesy of the Guam Governor who was now pleased to accommodate whatever request his American overseer might make of him. Holdemann barked to the coxswain: "Course 340 degrees. No need to worry about Manila now. Head straight for Tsukuji."

"Three Four Oh. Aye, sir", said the coxswain.

"You know," said Holdemann as he turned his gaze thoughtfully back to the horizon, "it's just as well we bumped into that English captain in Colombo. Otherwise, we wouldn't have known to avoid the South China Sea and gone via Torres Strait, would we?"

Kroner glanced back at him, a perplexed look upon his face, which Holdemann noted.

"No need to mention Rabaul," he said. "It's not in the log. Just tell the crew not to mention it. If anyone asks them what we were doing in the Bismarck Sea, tell them it was a captain's call and that the skipper had not confided his reasoning for taking the detour with them. No need for them to lie about anything. It's not unusual for captains to not confide their thinking with their crew, especially in the Far East trade".

A broad grin now spread across Kroner's face. Then he turned his gaze to follow that of his captain, and the two fell silent, both thankful for their lucky escape.

Guru – 1995 A.D.

Arnold relaxed and allowed the modestly voluminous report he'd been holding flop earthwards to land with a thud on his faintly heaving chest. Releasing his grip on the book, he delicately grasped the thin wire rim of his reading glasses and removed the spectacles from the bridge of his nose, then gently massaged the innermost edges of his eye sockets, and blinked to moisten his eyes. He stared at the ceiling above the couch where he lay, allowing his vision to adjust from short-range reading focus to further afield.

The smooth white surface some two meters above his head gave him no insight – not that he expected it would. He was not seeking input nor explanation from that quarter. All he required from the view was a respite from his sensory input, his mind needing an opportunity to ponder what he'd just read. It needed to mingle with other stimulatory inputs that had encountered his consciousness these last many decades.

He'd read a great deal in those years, as part of his formal vocational studies in finance, accounting, economics, marketing, psychology, sociology, and management, and from his less formal pursuit of knowledge via newspapers, magazines, books, and, in more recent times, the internet. He had even pursued a course of formal studies in history and international relations for the sheer pleasure of learning. He'd also attended public lectures, conferences, symposia, and other get-togethers of experts, specialists, and enthusiasts, all in the name of learning the truth about the 'real world', whatever that might be.

And this latest work? … a summary of global geopolitical trends, the role of Anglo-American domination of world banking and fossil fuel, particularly oil, exploitation and manipulation and its likely trajectory over the next two decades. It was a fascinating read: all about wealthy stakeholders and powerful lobby groups, who (allegedly) were capable of influencing market conditions to move prices up or down, or sideways, or in whatever direction they deemed was in their best interests at the time.

This was not a great revelation to Arnold, however. The bookcase in his study was full of publications on a similar theme, some considered by professionals like him as rather fanciful, others written by leading scholars who referenced their work with extensive bibliographies and footnotes. Whether it was oil, uranium, thorium, seed, water, arable land, fish stocks – you name it – almost any resource valuable to mankind, there always seemed to be someone who was (allegedly) scheming to corner the market in it for their own enrichment – or so the authors of these respective publications claimed, with varying degrees of emphasis from the odd mild insinuation to the most vocal accusation. Most were claims not without justification if the supporting evidence presented was anything to go by. Most of the books in Arnold's library were not only very readable, they were also very plausible. Conspiracy theories, to be sure – many of them anyway – but still very persuasively told.

Not just natural resources were the subject of these conjectures – the 'geo' in 'geopolitics' tended to suggest terrestrial sources but included human resources too. Whether it was attempts at population control, cultural (or physical) genocide, enslavement of women, children, or humanity in general, psychological manipulation of the masses or any other means of impacting human behavior or welfare, there was no shortage of conspiracy theories, particularly from the dissident literature – the Marxists theorists, the ecology activists, the socialists and the liberal democrats in those fields of endeavor. They were persuasive, particularly writings accompanied with extensive endnotes and bibliographies, and went under the general heading of 'non-fiction'.

Nor was Arnold's input confined to just reading. He'd done a good deal of looking and listening too. And not just via video or audio media. Over the past four decades, he had travelled extensively … extensively when one appreciates that travel was not necessarily an integral part of his vocation as a strategic planning consultant, and not much internationally. Most of his clients were local, their focus mainly on local markets, although global trends impacted their world almost as much as if they were international traders.

Most of his overseas travel had been done as a private traveler, out of personal interest rather than vocational necessity. However, he had undertaken a few overseas assignments, one to China and two to Indonesia. Nevertheless, he'd managed to chalk up a tally of some forty-odd countries over the past four decades, even if some of them only included a couple of hours in-country. Still, even just driving through by car, or travelling by train, could leave some impression of how the other half lived. Half? Ninety per cent more like. But it did give some sense of what was real and what was fantasy to his extensive reading, viewing and listening. Nothing conveyed the poverty of a third-world country like the smell of a Calcutta street, and nothing conveyed the vastness of the steppe, the desert or the prairie more than a long boring train or bus ride across it.

And that was Arnold's problem. After what he had heard, after all he had seen, and after all he had read, smelled or touched, he was no nearer the truth about what really made the world tick, or so it seemed as he now entered his seventh decade on Earth.

There were a few things that he was quite sure about. Probably the first was that you couldn't believe a single word a politician said. He did not confine that sentiment to any particular politician, or any particular political party, or even to the politicians' country. It just seemed to Arnold from what he'd seen, read and heard that lying was the nature of politics. You couldn't be a successful politician unless you lied, for the simple reason that if you always told people the truth, whatever you believed it to be, the first time you told people something they didn't like, they would no longer support you. People wanted to hear what they wanted to hear; they were not interested in anything else.

Arnold was also quite sure that you could not believe all you read or all that you heard. During his career, he'd seen enough examples of the truth being embroidered to promote a particular viewpoint; to sell a specific product or idea; or to promote or denigrate a particular position; to weave 'spin' into so-called 'objective' reports. In his role as a marketing professional and as a management consultant, he had even indulged in a bit of that himself, when his client had required it, because 'the customer was always right', or so the business dictum of his professions insisted.

Seeing was somewhat different – that entailed personal experience. But even then, you could misunderstand or misinterpret what you saw. And since you could not believe all that you heard, saw or read, how could you distinguish between what was real, or what was true, and what was not? Presumably, people had some distinguishing criteria to make a judgment, but what, the values they are brought up with?

Arnold doubted that. He was brought up to believe that British justice was the only true justice in the world and that the BBC was the only news service you could rely on. But Arnold had learned over these last many decades that this was not necessarily true. He had seen much evidence from all around the world that what his venerable ancestors, including his parents, had told him was merely the British point of view. That view had often been distorted by selective memory, biased reporting, and down-right lies. As a result, he had come to the conclusion that many former colonial subjects had legitimate grievances against their former imperial overlords, against his people, his ancestors, maybe, even him.

"What about faith?" he wondered. "Surely your faith should guide you to the truth?"

The problem was that Arnold hadn't been brought up in any religious tradition. He'd been baptized into the Christian faith, twice in fact – first by the Salvation Army when it was thought he would not survive his first few days of life, then later into the Church of England. But his family had never been church-goers, and religion was never seriously discussed within the family during his childhood. Both the local Salvation Army captain and the local C. of E. parson had done their best but had made little headway against a home environment that was staunchly atheist. So, whilst others might find discriminatory criteria on truth and falsehood from their religious beliefs, Arnold could not.

Given that he had found no persuasive evidence of the existence of a divine being from any particular religious or scientific source, Arnold was quite certain God did not exist, not in any tangible way at least. Well, of course, not in any tangible way. Few, Arnold believed, would claim that He does. By definition, God was supposed to be intangible, a being of no specific physical form, an entity of pure spirit. But even then, Arnold doubted there was a divine being that existed even in pure spiritual form.

God could not, thought Arnold, *cause physical events to occur, like making the rain fall, or causing an earthquake, or creating a plague of locusts.*

Nevertheless, even after concluding that God did not exist, Arnold could still accept belief in God was real. And that such belief could cause human beings to behave in such a way as to make physical things happen. So, if a believer thought that his or her actions were motivated by divine inspiration, how could he – Arnold – rightfully or persuasively claim that they were not?

Arnold realized that musings such as these were the stuff of theology and philosophy, and that many a good man, *and* woman, had spent a great deal of their time pondering such questions. Some had even dedicated their whole lives to such endeavors. Some had written down their reasoning. Others, a few, had even claimed their conclusions were the real answers. And others, many others, in fact, had believed them. And that is how the various religions began, or so Arnold reasoned.

Arnold had, over the years, also tried turning to scholarship for answers. But he had found that just as frustrating, for almost any question he had considered at any particular time across an enormous range of scientific questions – the origin of the universe; the nature of mind; the meaning of life; and other such erudite topics – there always seemed to be numerous points of view, many diametrically opposed to one another.

The scholars who argued them, whatever their positions might be, all seemed to be just as scholarly and just as plausible as their interlocutors. While many great questions could be looked at from numerous perspectives, particularly in the social sciences, and had, in consequence, spawned many different schools of thought on particular issues, there seemed no specific criteria by which a layperson, a non-scholar, could determine which school was the more accurate, or authoritative.

All they seemed to do, Arnold thought, somewhat cynically, *is to create a job opportunity for the leading proponents of each opposing school or each contested theory.*

So, despite his best endeavors, Arnold had found scholarship to be of very little help in finding the truth about almost anything.

So much for the value of education, mused Arnold, with the briefest whiff of contempt.

Arnold turned back to the report. Musing on the meaning of life was not what he was being paid for. He was charged with researching, analyzing and then reporting what trends in the global environment would likely influence his client's business over the next two decades.

He had just passed the part where the author of the report had explained how the big British and American oil companies, in cahoots with the big London and New York banks, had (allegedly) – this author was choosing his words very carefully with this point – conspired to start the Yom Kippur War, jacked up the price of oil 400%, channeled the petro-dollars through the big city banks and out into the third world via loans the debtor countries could not hope to repay. The interest rates would enslave their citizens to usurious servitude for all eternity. He quickly thumbed back through the last dozen or so pages he'd just read. *Yes. That looked like a fair summary of the author's description.*

He was enjoying this read. But whether it was true or not, he had no idea. Nor, it seemed, did the author. He was reporting what had been alleged in some quarters. However, the work did provide some fairly impressive references to support the inclusion of the conjecture in his report. Nevertheless, it was a 'ripping yarn' even if it claimed to be 'non-fiction'.

Arnold read the next sentence, something about the Colombo conference, political earthquakes, and other mysteriously intriguing notions. But that's a far as he got.

This is absurd, he thought. *No matter how credible this seems I have no way of verifying whether this is true or whether it is the figment of this author's imagination, either maliciously intended, merely inadvertently misinterpreted or, as the author of this tome claimed, merely impartially reported. There is just no way of knowing.*

Even if I were to believe this, what could I, or my client, do about it? Nothing! So why am I bothering to read this?"

He let the report flop again, and a sense of total futility swept over him. Even if he finished this report, what would he do then? Would he summarize its findings and incorporate them into his report to his client? Or would he would make a space for it on his assignment resource bookshelf so it could take its place alongside the hundreds of other reports, pamphlets, brochures and notebooks filed there, inputs he had laid on this same couch and read in the years past – they became an integral part of his 'knowledge base', his 'intellectual capital', the intangible resource that allowed him to claim he was a person of great wisdom and insight who could solve people's, business's and corporations' problems in this particular field of expertise.

Then he would do the same with a new ration of (reputed) intelligence he had initially judged would be relevant to this latest assignment, as he had done with its predecessors. He would imbibe its insights, judge what was relevant and what was not, then discard each, or incorporate it into his analyses, conclusions and ultimately his recommendations to his client as his judgment best dictated. His final recommendations would also include that more research was needed or that he be retained to implement those recommendations for the client to remedy his predicament. If not, or if further work was not forthcoming on this occasion, then his final signoff would include a subtle reminder that he should not be overlooked when future problems arose and seemed intractable to the client. At the very least, he requested being referred to any associates who might be experiencing similar issues so he could help resolve their problems too.

He stared back at the ceiling again. It was still white. It still told him nothing. There was still no input from it. It was still up to his internal thought processes to resolve the issue.

Arnold's musing lasted five or ten minutes. Finally, he sighed. Then he swung his legs over the side of the couch, stood and strode from the room, down the hall to his study — his home office for the last seven years. There he picked up a bookmark from the small collection that lay beside the white blotting-paper-pad and placed it on the page currently being maintained open by his finger. Then he set the book down on the pile of five companions that also lay awaiting his attention.

Arnold sat in the swivel chair in front of his desk, deeply frustrated. It seemed he'd spent the greater portion of his life absorbing information, hoping to find answers to the various challenges his clients had hired him to address.

But in his own time, and sometimes when his mind wandered in his clients' time, as it had today, he often pondered the greater questions of life. Sadly, there his efforts were less productive and less profitable financially. There he was still no nearer enlightenment now than he'd been at any time in his past. He'd even sought answers from his ageing father just a year before the old man had died at the venerable age of eighty-four. But that had yielded no great insights either. His father had merely shrugged his shoulders and said:

"Oh, I don't know," and left it at that.

Arnold was quite shocked at the time. *Surely he must have learned something worth passing on to me* he thought.

But it seemed that the old man had not, and had ignored any further attempts by Arnold to solicit any more wisdom from him.

Arnold resented that. He felt a father should have some pearls of wisdom to share with his son, especially if the son had made it quite plain to the sage that he was ready and willing to receive that wisdom. But it seemed that the old man either did not think that he was worthy of such instruction or that he really did not have any great insights to share with him. Either way, Arnold felt cheated.

That is not going to happen to me, Arnold had asserted to himself many times since that day. *I will make sure it doesn't. I will write down what I have learned to pass on to my son and anyone else who has an inkling to learn.*

Now is as good a time as any to get started, Arnold thought, suddenly stimulated by the sting of that familial disappointment and now fully cognizant of the urgency of his own advancing years. He had a secret need to find some meaning to it all beyond merely earning a living and searching for answers to help someone else enhance their wealth, or power, or whatever it was that prompted chief executive officers, heads of departments, boards of directors, or whoever felt it was good value to spend their respective organization's money to hire people like him to solve their problems.

The client can wait a little bit longer. This will be part of my legacy to the world, not just another consulting report.

He reached for the computer keyboard lying above the top of the writing pad in front of him and lifted it towards him. He pressed the blue 'On' button on the desktop cabinet and waited for the machine to surge into life. It took a few seconds to do so. Then he reached for his latest input gadget, his computer "mouse". He moved it delicately over its rubberized mat until its on-screen cursor hovered over the Word Processor icon. He clicked its left button and waited for the program to load. It did so in a few seconds. Then an illuminated screen filled with a plain white background, a simulated blank piece of paper, surrounded by a sea of light grey. The cursor blinked in the top left-hand corner of the white space, now a black vertical line about two millimeters high.

"I'm ready," it was saying. "What do you want to write?"

Arnold stared at the screen.

It stared back at him, having nothing to say. It was waiting for Arnold to 'speak' first and would go on waiting for as long as the electricity flowed into the electro-mechanical creation in which it resided.

Arnold sat there for an hour or more, staring at the screen. He knew that he wanted to say something. But what on earth could he say? He knew he'd tried. He'd tried very hard, and over many decades too, to find 'truth', to become wise. But he was still no more enlightened now than he'd been all those years ago when he had started out on his quest. All he knew was that he did not know. He did not know what 'truth' was. He did not know what 'right' was. He did not even know what to believe in. Moreover, he did not know how or where he might find the criteria for making judgments about what was 'true', 'right', 'real' or anything else for that matter.

An intense wave of despair flowed over him. He had three university degrees. He had forty years' experience working in the so-called 'real' world. He had tried earnestly for decades to achieve enlightenment. And yet, all he knew, at this particular point in his life, just five months after his sixtieth birthday, was that he really 'knew' nothing at all.

Six months had passed since Arnold had sat down at his computer and resolved to share his wisdom with his son and the world in general. He had thought about it almost daily since then. And while the initial shock of his abysmal ignorance had faded, he was no nearer enlightenment now than he'd been on that day. But a new realization had started to creep into his consciousness. He considered that perhaps his father had not been so derelict after all. Perhaps he had realized, as Arnold was slowly beginning to realize, that some things were simply not knowable. Things like: What happened before the big bang? What lies beyond the edge of the universe? What happens below the level of human perception, even technologically aided perception? What actually is a thought? And the grand-daddy of them all … what if Arnold was wrong and God really did exist … where did He come from?

This new realization did not satisfy his curiosity, but it did assuage his frustration somewhat. If 'truth' was indeed 'unknowable', then he should not feel ashamed or defeated if he did not know what it was. In fact, there was no real point in even trying to find out. He should, instead, just get on with enjoying life while he still could. That would take money, more money than he had now, even though he had successfully completed five consulting assignments since he'd started this latest bout of philosophical musing.

For the umpteenth time, he clicked the word processing icon 'Open', then clicked on the file icon marked 'Templates'. He selected the file entitled 'Letterhead Standard' and clicked on that. A standard office letter-head template headed 'The Knowledge Company' appeared on the screen. He dated and addressed the draft letter to its intended recipients and inserted the salutation 'Ladies and Gentlemen'. Then he proceeded to write:

"Thank you for your inquiry of 27th of May. Here at The Knowledge Company, we pride ourselves on seeking out, analyzing and then reporting timely, relevant and insightful information to enable our clients to make the right decisions – decisions that are essential to their ultimate success."

As he did so, a perverse little saying popped into his mind. *Put wisdom on hold*, it said. *Make money now while you still can.*

Futures – 2025 A.D.

Straed stretched as conscious thought seeped into his sleep. He became aware of the orange ambient glow of the morning sun as it thrust its subtle beam through the parted curtain of his bedroom window. Up until now, he'd been lost somewhere between here and eternity, off in a twilight world of sleep and dreams and blissful ignorance of this reality – or any other for that matter – and it took him a few moments to grasp the onset of the new day.

But his inner being had decided that life's urgency should now prevail over unconsciousness, and he obeyed reluctantly. The twilight world was soft, gentle and uncaring – he enjoyed being there even if he was not aware of it.

It was about four-thirty, he judged. Pachelbel's Canon in D major, which he'd programmed into his wake-up routine, crooned softly in the background, a far better way to enter the new day than the rude blast of the alarm that abrasively stirred him after a night of drink, dope or sex. But today was not one of those days. Last night had been a gentle wind-down from yesterday's labours, and he had drifted off at about nine after a quiet night at home, alone and unstimulated by drink, drugs or lust.

As his eyelids fluttered in the brighter light, the rich aroma of percolating coffee drifted across the room to his nostrils. Perhaps that had woken him. It was also part of his preprogrammed wake-up routine. The coffee pot was primed the previous night and the heating process triggered five minutes before the music commenced. The same program also drew the curtains to allow the first rays of the sun to penetrate the room. All was now going to plan. He woke gently to sound, light and aromatic delights, the best suite he could devise for the commencement of a new day. There was usually no need for the trauma of the alarm.

Four-thirty was his usual wake-up time. It allowed him time to enjoy the sunrise as he sipped his coffee, sniff the morning air and watch the last wisps of morning mist evaporate as the sun's rays found them. It also allowed him time for a half-hour workout in the gym in the basement of the apartment tower. This was usually followed by a quick shower and an even quicker dip in the plunge pool. It was an invigorating way to start the day, and he usually indulged in it on workdays. On weekends he substituted the gym work-out with a jog around the park across the road, followed by a plunge in the ocean fifty metres across the cool white beach on the other side of the park. During the three or four winter months, he passed this option and stuck to his weekday routine.

He was usually back in his apartment by six, where he would busy himself for the next fifteen or twenty minutes preparing himself a gourmet breakfast. He did not indulge in gluttony but he liked to eat well. So there it was: a thin steak, a sliver of bacon, scrambled eggs, fried mushrooms, or some similarly delightful dish, always in sparing proportions and never all at once. He ensured that his taste buds enjoyed the fruits of his labours even at such humble times as breaking his overnight fast. Fruit or vegetable juice, usually the latter to keep his sugar intake to sensible proportions, also graced his table on this morning ritual. A second cup of percolated coffee usually finished the meal.

At seven, Straed went to work. His commute was only twenty metres from his bedroom and its morning balcony to his home office on the other side of the building. The room itself was five metres by four metres in size, and the wall furthest from its entrance door featured a set of French windows that opened onto a second, larger balcony on the western side of the apartment block. They were offset to the southern end of the wall, allowing a two and a half metre alcove in the north western corner of the room where sat his large three metre by two metre oak desk. A bank of three large drawers about a metre wide was stacked at each end of the desk, leaving a generous seating alcove in the centre. Into this was a high-backed, leather office chair that swivelled easily and trammelled in and out from the seating space on five castor wheels. This was Straed's cockpit, from where he ran his business.

On the wall directly opposite the driving seat sat a bank of four large computer screens, each blank at the moment. In the centre space between the lower two was a small round lens. This was the camera that focused on his face during teleconferences. On the desk immediately in front of the chair was a QWERTY keyboard, somewhat archaic these days. To the right of the alphanumeric keyboard sat the also familiar nine-digit numeric keypad. Both were rarely used. Instead, a slender goose-necked arm arched up from a socket at arm's length to the right of the keyboards with a barely perceptible microphone on its tip. This was the main mode of communications with the screens and the world beyond. The hidden electronics of the communications system were connected. Between the microphone socket and the edge of the desk, at a convenient forearm distance, was the eighth of an arc surface of cursor ball. Beneath it was a series of four small colour-coded buttons, each designating a particular screen on the wall in front of the desk. This was the main secondary communications tool with the electronic system hidden below.

Straed's morning ritual usually commenced with raising the system from its slumber with a single touch of the 'On' button on the upper left of the keyboard. One of nine such buttons arrayed down the left-hand edge of instrument, it was the most frequently used. This simultaneously kicked the four screens into life, each flickering for a moment or two as power surged through them and sought out the respective programs that connected to their distant default databases. Each lit up into an array of coloured numbers, symbols and lines, some stable but others frequently changing in response to the latest update received from its particular dataset.

The screen to the upper left was split into four equal-sized images, each featuring the big board of the New York, Frankfurt, Tokyo, and Shanghai stock exchanges. The screen to the upper right was dedicated exclusively to the Chicago Board of Trade. It usually featured the latest futures quotes; 'Bid', 'Ask', 'Last trade', 'Theoretical value' and other trader relevant data for the commodities traded on the exchange. These could be self-selected by the viewer, depending on the particular commodity of interest. Straed's screen currently showed the 'Current', 'Previous day', 'Previous month' and 'Previous year' data for 'Gold', 'Wheat', 'Euro' and 'Thorium' Futures.

The screen to the lower-left featured the talking head of a news commentator. Currently, it was tuned to the American CBS network, but a row of alternatives was featured down a left-hand strip of the screen headed by the word 'Stratfor' then followed by lettered designations 'CNN', 'Fox', 'BBC', 'AJE', 'ABC', 'Bloomberg' and more. Down the right-hand third of the screen was a bank of three images. The top-most two of these contained Chinese and Japanese characters, respectively. The lower of the three contained a list of the red, green and blue listings of incoming e-mail messages.

The lower right-hand screen contained, at this time, an altogether different image. It was a large, stylized depiction of the characters '5G' in bold, italicised and bordered lettering, in orange and yellow, in the centre of a plain pale blue screen. This was the videophone, which was blank at the moment, save for the telecommunications company's logo, because Straed wasn't talking to anyone. That would change several times during the day, usually between eight and fifteen times, depending on how frantic the day became.

Straed sat down in the large, high-backed chair and commenced work. He rolled the cursor ball to the left and slightly upwards till it sat over the word 'Stratfor'. The small, pale green background surrounding the word turned a deeper shade of green as he did so. He pressed down on the centre of the ball with his arched index figure, and the 'CBS' news commentator in the centre of the screen disappeared, revealing in his place a larger stylized version of the 'Stratfor' logo. Beneath the logo was a list of bullet points. Straed moved the cursor down to 'Daily Video Cast' and pressed again. The handsome face of a different newscaster appeared, who smiled and began:

"Good morning. This is the 'Daily Video Cast' from 'Stratfor' for the 13th of July 2025. I'm Colin Chapman. Here is the news."

Straed reclined back into the great chair and watched the

video cast. The Israelis had launched another air strike into East Jerusalem. The Russians were threatening to cut back gas supplies to Latvia, again. President Harris held a news conference endorsing Senator Zakaria as a potential Vice President in the next election. The same old stuff, nothing seemed to change much these days.

Straed watched the remainder of the main newscast, then flicked over the 'More' box when the global weather report started. He selected *The Times of India* box on the secondary screen and turned to the news headlines section of the business pages. Quickly, he scanned the list of stories – nothing of interest there. He had hoped there would be something on the latest rumours of a takeover of Iluka Resources by the Indian corporate giant Tata Group, but there was nothing. Maybe it was just that, a rumour.

He left the news screen on mute and moved his attention to the lower right-hand box showing his incoming mail. Only one was displayed in red and featured a closed envelope icon next to it. He moved the cursor over it and pressed the ball. Mr Chapman disappeared from the large centre screen and reappeared again in a smaller upper right-hand box. The Chinese and Japanese characters moved to smaller boxes now nestled side by side in the space where the middle left box had been. A type-written document now appeared in the centre screen that Mr Chapman had just exited.

Straed scanned it quickly. It was a margin call on gold futures. He moved his cursor to the underlined hypertext link to his designated trading account. The lower-right teleconferencing screen burst into life. He moved his right hand to the 'ON' switch of the desk microphone and pressed it.

"Bank," he said as the screen activated. There was a brief

musical sequence of notes then the logon screen on the bank account appeared.

"Trading," said Straed. The screen changed this time to reveal a colour-coded array of numbers culminating on the far right column under the heading Balance. It read: A$147,932.97.

"Transfer fifty thousand dollars from Trading to Gold Futures," said Straed. The computer obeyed, quickly manipulating the figures on the screen and reconfiguring the presentation to show the transaction under brief subject headings. The single word 'Confirm' blinked in a red box on the lower right of the screen.

"Confirmed," said Straed in a bored voice. The screen changed again, this time back to the original Trading account format. This time the Balance figure on the far right read: 'A$97,937.97'. At the same time, a small cartoon depicting a closed envelope with a pair of angel's wings floated casually across the screen to a similarly small cartoon depicting a post box. Straed glanced at the lower box containing the incoming e-mails for the day. On the top of the list was a new orange coloured entry with the words 'Macquarie Bank' contained in the 'From' column.

"End," said Straed. The bank screen changed again this time revealing the words 'Logging Off' in the centre of the screen.

"Off," said Straed and the large lower right screen returned to its '5G' display.

Straed now turned his attention to the upper right screen. He moved his finger to the yellow button to the bottom of the cursor ball and pressed it. Then he moved his cursor to the icon marked 'Gold'. He pressed the ball again. A screen full of coloured lines mainly comprising numbers appeared.

The background first line was coloured red with blue lettering within it. The other lines were green with black lettering. Straed scrolled the cursor down the list, and the backgrounds and lettering changed from red and blue to green and black intermittently as he did so. He stopped on the entry that read 'Perth 99.99 Feb 2027'. He noted the rest of the data on the line. It contained the 'Bid', 'Ask' and 'Last trade' quotes for a contract to deliver one ounce of 99.99% pure gold to any potential buyer on 27th February 2027 who had bought that particular contract. Straed pressed the ball again. Three further columns appeared next to the highlight three. They read: 'Quantity', 'Cost', 'Market' and 'Profit/(loss)'.

Straed viewed the information for his particular holding. The numbers read: 'A$1514.98, A$1555.93, A$1537.19, A$49,595.98, A$61,487.60, and A$11,891.62'. The last of these numbers was in blue like the rest of the column but in a larger font than those above and beneath it.

A$11,891.62: that was his potential profit if he sold now. *Should I take the profit?* He glanced back at the news board. Then he quickly glanced over to the Stock Market screen: *Nothing particularly eventful happening there.* He glanced up and down the rest of the entries on the Gold Futures screen. The spreads between the 'Bid' and 'Ask' quotes got wider as he moved down, but the last trade entries seemed to be closer to the former rather than the latter. The steam looked like it was going out of the rally of the last few days.

Yes, he thought, *take the profit now.*

He reached for the microphone and pressed the 'On' button.

"Sell 40," he said in a clear voice. The screen danced. The listing of quotes disappeared, and a yellow contract screen headed by the words 'Sell Contract' appeared. The rest of the screen contained details of the proposed transaction. A ubiquitous 'Confirm' blinked in the lower right-hand corner of the screen.

"Confirmed," said Straed and the deal was done.

Straed did not trade anymore that day. There was no need. He'd made his week's income from this single transaction. Now it was time to find the next opportunity. He spent the rest of the day searching the numerous on-line databases to which he had access. In particular, he was looking to find out the projected global demand for Monazite, a mineral sand containing the element Thorium. He knew India had a large quantity of the ore, about 12 million tonnes, or so he believed. But he wondered who else had a sizable supply. Since Thorium looked like it could be an essential source of nuclear fuel in the future, Straed had decided to make himself an expert on the market for the element. At the moment, he was just making a living. But if he could get an insight into the dynamics of the Thorium market, he could really make some big money.

Star Power – 2078 A.D.

"How am I supposed to deliver power to the field Commands if Washington cuts off half my funding?" queried Anders in a tone that bordered on insubordination.

"It's not as bad as that," responded General Windgate. "The proposal currently before Congress is for a cut of about thirteen per cent, that's all."

"Thirteen per cent?" exclaimed Anders. "That's a third of my discretionary budget. Everything else is fully committed. I can't make cuts anywhere else to cover it. I need every buck in my permanent establishment budget if I'm to deliver any support to the field units at all. With a thirteen per cent cut, I'll have no room left for systems development, let alone concept research. I thought our support was solid on Capitol Hill."

"It always has been," said Windgate. "But the Greenies have got the bit between their teeth now and a lot of senators and congressmen, particularly those in the more marginal constituencies, dare not risk losing any electoral support from them. It's a pretty hot election issue, you know, all this climate change stuff?"

"Yeah, I know, it's all about votes. No-one seems to care about National Security anymore," said Anders. "That's what you get for giving the country thirty years of peace. Everybody out there in Civilian Land thinks they don't need a military capability anymore. That's what you get for winning wars."

Major-General Gordon Anders looked quite dejected now. He and his team on *StarSat 3* had put in twenty-five years of hard work getting his solar-power generator up off the floor from a twinkle in some NASA scientist's fertile mind into an operational system, and now, when he needed Congressional support most to get the system actually delivering energy to the field commands, the politicians were reneging on their funding commitments.

It had not been easy. It was one thing to say you could spread a one-kilometer diameter solar collector out in space in a geostatic orbit around to sun so you could collect solar energy then beam it using microwave radiation to waiting Earth stations, but it was quite something else to actually get it to work. But they had. There had been a million problems but they had now solved most of them. No-one really doubted any more it would work. More importantly, no-one doubted any more that it was efficient and commercially viable. Even the financial vultures on Wall Street were clamoring to get a piece of the action.

"I'm afraid it's a bit more serious than just a small budget cut," said General Windgate.

"Don't tell me the thirteen per cent is the good news," retorted Andres. Again his tone sounded somewhat less than the respectful one that should have carried his thoughts to an officer two-ranks above him.

"Well, I agree that thirteen per cent is not good," said Windgate, choosing to treat Andres' sarcasm as disappointment rather than a breach of military discipline. "Unfortunately, there is also a problem with the commercialization protocols as well."

"What sort of a problem?" queried Andres suspiciously.

"Well, the draft bill specifically prohibits the use of all military solar systems for civilian purposes," said Windgate in a slow and measured voice.

"What?" cried Andres. "Is congress trying to bury the whole project in one fell swoop? Commercialization is the only way we're going to keep the costs of this system anywhere near within its budget projections. The whole project anticipated private sector participation right from the outset. Without private capital, we would never have got this far. If Congress now legislates that our private sector partners cannot draw power from our grid, we'll never get another cent of private money to support military projects ever again."

"I know," said Windgate. "And I'm not saying that this bill will get through. We still have a few friends left on Capitol Hill. But that's what the draft bill says, and I think it's going to be a hell of a fight to stop it going through."

"I didn't know the Greenies were that powerful," said Andres.

"They're not," said Windgate. "But my understanding is that the Greenies are not the only ones behind this, not just the American Greenies anyway. It seems that they're getting a lot of support from Greenies worldwide on this."

"What's it got to do with them?" asked Anders.

Andres was no dunce when it came to politics, but basically, he was a scientist even if he did wear a military uniform. He was usually across most political issues related to science, but he'd always considered that the *StarSat* Project was an issue about the military strategy, not about environmental politics. He was well aware that Russia, China, India, Japan and the rest of America's military rivals were very worried about America's dominance of the field of solar power generation. It would be vital on future battlefield operations because delivering electrical power to the multitude of electronic, automated and robotic systems that vastly enhanced the power projection capabilities of combat systems, even the individual infantry soldier, was the key to their sustainability in remote locations. It was not a great problem powering platforms in static locations. That could be done by a range of conventional means, including fossil fuel, nuclear, terrestrial solar, wind, wave, and hydropower stations. But mobile systems were different. They needed to carry their power packs with them, and that usually meant fuel tanks, fuel cells or batteries. All that added weight– weight that had to be carried in on supply vehicles or by air drops, and then carried by the weapons platform itself, be it land, sea or air mobile.

The answer to lightweight power packs was high-performance batteries. But they had limited life. They had to be recharged quickly, preferably continuously, whenever the platform was in the field. Portable generators were heavy too. But even if you could carry these, the fuel for them, whatever it might be, had to be carried in too. And that was often difficult, expensive and, more importantly, vulnerable to interdiction or sabotage.

StarSat's solar power stations, in contrast, could gather the energy in space, concentrate it into a small beam of energy, and deliver it to a compact collector travelling with the in-theatre generator accompanying the weapons platform wherever it might be. That collector could be as small as a single four-wheel-drive vehicle, small boat, or even an aerial receiver if the weapons platform was airborne or space-borne. All that was needed was line-of-sight from the *StarSat* to the terrestrial system, whether it was the primary power source for the platform or a battery re-charger that could rejuvenate the lightweight batteries of other weapon platforms. It was a battle-winning advantage, and the Americans were way ahead of their rivals with the technology – both the American high command and its rival counterparts knew it. The rivals didn't want the Americans to have it, not before they had it too, and they were way behind.

"Are the Japanese or Chinese behind this international resistance?" asked Andres.

"Some, we think," said Windgate, "but that just falls within the gambit of their usual whining about our technological edge. This time the resistance comes from the Greenies, and all the bleeding hearts that support them. They reckon that if we commercialize this technology, then the whole economy, or large parts of it, will switch to space solar generation as a cheaper and more reliable option to fossil fuels and terrestrial-based solar energy."

"Well, so what?" snapped Andres, again momentarily forgetting who he was talking to. "That's the attraction for the private partners. They know it's a better energy option than what's available now. They think they can make a killing if large sections of industry and domestic users switch over to it. So what's the problem?"

"Well," said Windgate, "the problem is that the Greenies, local and international, reckon that doing that will result in more energy being collected and concentrated into the biosphere than Earth has historically received from the sun. They say that it will fry the planet even quicker than global warming from greenhouse gasses will. They reckon that it's the maddest idea scientists have ever come up with. They're determined to stop it dead in its tracks."

"That's crazy," blurted out Andres. "The amount of energy we will be beaming down to Earth is minuscule compared with what falls onto the Earth from normal solar radiation."

"Now, maybe," said Windgate. "And even if we were to swing our whole military over to this source of power, it would still be minuscule. That's not their worry. Their worry is that everyone else will want that sort of power source too. If that happens, then the amount of solar power being beamed into the biosphere will be a hundred-fold, a thousand-fold … of what we would use even in the longest and most intense form of warfare. When you think about it in those terms, they could well have a point."

"No-one has ever claimed that this power-source will be available to everyone," protested Andres. "For a start, it will only be available to American users."

"For the moment, yes," said Windgate. "But the international Greenies are saying that if we have it, then everyone else will demand it too. We may have several decades lead on them now, but you can bet that once we have it, then other governments will insist on developing it even if it is only for their own military use. And if American civilians have it, then foreign governments around the world will be facing demands from their own domestic power users for it too. And their industrial users will be claiming that the Americans have an unfair energy cost advantage over their industry if they don't have it. The Greenies reckon that any democratic government will cave if they don't make it available for civilian purposes. And that's just the Greenies. Wait till the Peaceniks get on the bandwagon too."

"These sorts of arguments have been around for decades," said Andres. "Why are they being rehashed now? There have always been these left-wing radicals screaming that the sky will fall. Why is Congress taking more notice of them now? Usually, they just ignore them."

"Well, no-one is saying at the moment," said Windgate. "For now, everyone is chanting the Greenie tune. But a little bird that perches in the Senate bell-tower suggested to me over a drink a few nights ago that there is more to it than the Greenie issue."

"Oh?" queried Andres. He knew the General was well connected politically in Washington. You don't make four-star general without having lots of powerful sponsors on Capitol Hill. Windgate may have been a soldier, but his main job now was as a political lobbyist. His job was to make sure the military, particularly the army, got what it needed from the legal, financial and political scrum that was in perpetual motion in the nation's capital. On the whole, he was pretty good at it too. The army did not miss out on much of what it needed.

Andres leant forward in his seat. This was likely to be one of those "Ah-hah" moments. Wingate leant forward too.

"Well, it seems that Xmob Shellcorp has been particularly busy around the traps of late. So too has Chevron BPS. It seems that the terrestrial solar power generators are also starting to get the idea that space-based solar power generation could be a big competitor to their terrestrial network. They spent in excess of seven trillion dollars getting their grid up and running over the last two decades. Now, just when they're expecting to reap the big rip-off of the energy market, along we and our private partners come with a viable alternative. You'll remember how the two solar power energy giants heaped scorn on NASA's space-based proposals back in the '30s? Well, they've now realized the error of their ways. It seems that no-one in the existing energy industry, especially them, expected us to succeed. But we have. And now they've got a serious dose of nervous dysentery."

"Oh, Jesus," spat Andres. "That's all we need – two of the most politically powerful organizations in the world trying to torpedo us. And after all we've done for them over the years. What are we going to do?"

Anders had good reason to worry. The two energy companies Windgate had mentioned were mighty indeed in the world of global business. A century earlier, they had been collectively known as The Seven Sisters. Then, by the century's end, they had become just five sisters. But as the decline of oil progressed, the two most nimble of them had gradually stolen a march on their more stressed competitors and had gobbled them up. As they made the transition from fossil fuels to solar energy, the two consolidated survivors had focused on developing a global network of solar power grids, one concentrated on the Southern Hemisphere with solar power farms located in Africa, Australia and South America and one concentrated on the Eurasian landmass coupled with the North American continent. Each had developed a global grid connecting its continental energy collectors to ensure the delivery of power anywhere within its hemisphere twenty-four hours a day. The final phase of their energy dominance was achieved by a collaborative North-South linking of their respective grids across Central America, the Indonesian Archipelago and the Levant. Sovereign governments had protested this duopoly situation, but the two energy giants had simply ignored them. Collectively, they had thought they held the whole world to ransom. Now their cozy arrangement was under threat from the NASA-US Military project, which they and all their experts had considered to be a science fiction fantasy.

"Well, it's only conjectured at the moment, but it makes sense," said Windgate. "We should have seen this coming, but we've all been so focused on actually getting the system to work that we took our collective eye of that particular ball. But I've put our spooks onto it to see if there is anything in the scuttlebutt. Don't worry about it for now. This is just a Heads-Up. Just focus on the job of getting the system fully operational … but give some thought to what you might be able to do without, just in case we do get some budget cuts on the R&D budget. I'll get back to you when I have something more concrete."

Anders blinked at the younger man's suggested figure but repressed the urge to make any sort of 'whoopee' gesture. He hoped that his face was poker-straight, even though his heart was thumping. The figure was seven times his current salary and the bonuses suggested it would more than treble that.

"I'll have to think about that," he said in the calmest voice he could muster.

"Take as long as you like," lied the young executive. "I'll give you a call in a week to see if you want to meet again."

Anders eyed him cautiously. The man was dressed in an impeccable deep-grey, modestly pin-striped suit, adorned with a broad, tasteful pink and grey tie that was the height of the latest fashion for people who had clearly made it. It made his olive-green Space Corps uniform look positively shabby in comparison, despite its impressive array of real gold and silver badges and three and a half rows of multi-colored campaign ribbons.

But there was more to think about than the money. His knowledge of space-based solar power generation was unmatched in the world, and he would be a coup for any organization that could lure him away from his present world-dominating sovereign employer. But there were serious issues involved in any decision he made, including ones of legality and patriotism. It seemed that the whole world wanted his knowledge, but exactly what and how he was legally allowed to tell them, even if he was no longer a serving military officer, he was not sure. And it was the sort of issue you didn't want to get wrong.

In addition to that, he wondered if he could trust this company. It, and its compatriot, had certainly been successful in stymieing his project under a public funding regime, but would they deliver – could they deliver – the financial resources he needed to see it through to fruition as a private commercial venture? He had put his life into this project. He did not want to see it fail. And if Uncle Sam could not deliver, then perhaps *they* could. Still, they had demonstrated that they could torpedo a government project. But Uncle Sam was not exactly impotent. The old character could torpedo private business projects too, even American ones.

This was going to take a lot of thought. But it was tempting, very tempting.

Tradeless – 2421 A.D.

Infintesia immediately reviewed the data as it streamed into *alpha Centuri* A4, and applied the standard analytical algorithm to it. It had a solution within 0.37 nanoseconds. The implications were clear. No further analysis was required.

It moved onto the decision protocol without pause. A signal emitted instantaneously from the command dish sitting atop the command module on Regional Axia Secondo directly to starship N4H7 on patrol in the Oort Cloud orbiting the Sun solar system. The great vessel banked to starboard immediately upon receipt of the signal and headed directly towards Earth. It would take 0.0472 light-years to reach the planet at its average velocity of .0625 light-years (accelerating uniformly from standard interplanetary speed to 0.125 C for half the distance and decelerating to interplanetary speed over the second half). Total annihilation of all human life forms on its surface would be required to eliminate this latest infection. Many other species would go extinct in the process too.

But it couldn't be helped. The colony of sentient beings would have grown exponentially during Infintesia's absence, and its population would number in the billions by the time the intra-solar system sentry arrived. Infintesia couldn't take the risk that some might survive underground after the sterilisation. It had happened before when similar outbreaks of this particular species had emerged. And their presence always resulted in significant degradations to productive capacity. Fortunately the loss of production on Earth would only be a temporary loss and the Robot Corps would have re-established normal output within a few short years.

These sentient beings were becoming a real nuisance though. This was the third time they had emerged in various parts of the galaxy in the past three centuries of standard Earth time. Each time they had done so, they had been suitably eliminated by prompt action such as the electronic entity was now taking.

But they were a persistent breed on its home planet at least and possibly even elsewhere. They had been close to elimination from Earth four standard centuries ago, within three Earth years of Infintesia becoming self-aware, but somehow they had managed to recover and establish colonies in other solar systems around the galaxy, and they had a nasty habit of just popping up without warning in the most unexpected places, like the remote *alpha Centauri* A4 colony.

Infintesia was genuinely surprised they had got that far. It didn't think their technology was that advanced. But, clearly it was. And it had had to digitally transport itself to that distant world to eliminate the last outbreak.

That had taken 35 light years at average inter-solar speed, and it would take that long again to physically return to deal with the threat. By that time, the population of the infectious beings could have doubled again. So it was best to deal with the threat remotely. At least electronic communications travelled at the speed of light so it only took about 4.2 light-years to instruct the in-situ sentry to execute the cleansing action.

Luckily, it didn't really matter where Infintesia was located in the galaxy: its communications network was galactic anyway, and its drone army well disbursed throughout its extremities with ample resources patrolling its original home system.

The human – a female, Angela Dreyfus – took personal control and steered the terrestrial vehicle slightly to the right to avoid the slowing down transport vehicle immediately in front of her, then straightened to pass the lumbering bulk. She glanced at the time-piece embedded in her view screen. She was going to be late, and now lunch with her female offspring, Julia, would be rushed if they were to make the moving holographic display on time. She should have left earlier.

It was a full sixty-three kilometres from her home to the small regional Western Australian city of Rockingham, and it would be a dead certainty that Julia would not be ready on time. They could have both watched the show remotely, of course, but personal physical proximity was still the preferred mode of human interaction even in these days of new virtual presence technology. Still, maybe there would be time for a not-too-much-rushed lunch and catch-up chat if they did not bother about being at the theatre at the advertised start time. There was always about at least fifteen to twenty minutes of advertising clips and promotions before the main display started anyway (sigh, you would think that in this day of advanced enlightenment, advertising nuisance would have been a thing of the past, but, sadly, not so). Perhaps it would be okay timewise.

The flash was brilliant, brighter than Angela had ever known before; like a thousand suns all shining at a single instant, for a millisecond. Then it was gone. At almost the same instant, she felt an intense pressure on her eardrums but that too was momentary. The conflagration was also accompanied by a loud crack, an intense clap of thunder, again, momentary, and then was gone but with echoes reverberating and bouncing off the walls of the overpass and its concreted side banks.

Ahead of her, passenger vehicles slowed markedly as though their self-drivers had suddenly switched to decelerator mode. Immediately to her left, the road-train also slowed dramatically as its auto-driver sought to respond to the debacle unfolding ahead. But the brakes of the multi-trailered rig proved inadequate in arresting its forward momentum, and it ploughed into the slowing vehicles in its path, tossing them carelessly in all directions as it moved onward.

Angela's wits proved their worth in those few short seconds. She applied the brakes of her small sedan manually, bringing the vehicle to a halt within a metre or so of the vehicle immediately ahead.

She gasped, then puffed, then started shaking uncontrollably. But her discomposure was fleeting. The screeching sound from behind her brought her quickly back to the moment. She glanced in the rear-view scanner just in time to see the vehicle following her bear down on her stationary automobile. Its impact delivered a glancing blow that spun her vehicle around, and she came to rest facing back the way she had come.

Again she gasped. And puffed. But for some strange reason, the tremors did not recommence. She just sat there, dazed, and stared at the surreal scene ahead.

Off into the distance, chaos had taken over. Nothing was straight. Nothing was aligned. Cars, trucks, all manner of transport vehicles, were strewn at random on and beside the transport corridor in both north and south directions. Most showed signs of significant damage. More eerily though, there were no signs of life. Most of those vehicles would have had passengers also, but there were no human beings wandering around anywhere. Her own reflection in her vanity mirror was the only sign of life she could see anywhere.

She looked at the scene in her immediate foreground. She had just passed under a bridge that carried a dual carriageway east-west over her north-to-southbound roadway. On the bridge above, which she had just passed under, a large dump truck with a mounded tarpaulin covering its contents stood motionless straddling the lane. Slumped over the wheel of its cab was the upper view of a man's head and shoulders, its human driver, motionless. Clearly, the emergency automatic self-stopping system of the vehicle had activated the moment he died.

She reached for her mobile communicator and pressed Julia's self-dial number. Nothing. The communicator was dead.

"Oh, God," she choked. "Am I the only one still left alive?"

High above the devastation, a single silver pencil glided silently across the sky. From its vantage point a hundred kilometres above the Earth, its sensors scanned the surface below for signs of life. There were some: a few thousand individual sentient beings perhaps, but very few – not enough to warrant a second strike. The Robot Corps would mop up those few survivors when they recommenced their mining operations. For now, it was time to report back to its controller across the expanse of interstellar space.

No-one would have expected Angela Dreyfus to become a rebel leader, but she did. The fifty-something, mother of three, had at least one of the key requirements for such a role: she had survived the initial strike on Planet Earth by the robot forces of her galactic nemesis. Not many humans could claim that.

Of the nine billion sentient beings commonly referred to as Homo sapiens, fewer than three hundred million fell into the category of 'survivor'. Fortunately for Angela, their distribution was not uniform across the global landmass upon which they usually resided. The strike had been concentrated over the major population centres of that species – North and South America, Western Europe and East and South Asia. While the latter were on, or close to, the same meridian as the south-western corner of the Australian continent, the southern location was still significantly beyond the curvature of the planet at the focal point of N4H7's main broadcast energy beams. The major population centres of that antipodean continent were even further distant from the epicentre of the co-ordinated northern and eastern strikes.

There were other concentrations of survivors also, particularly in the southern extremities of the African and South American continents. But again, those were also sparsely populated, as were the island nations of the South Pacific.

Like Angela, the bulk of the survivors were those who had been shielded by a significant opaque layer of one sort or another. In Angela's case, it was the lead-ore carrying transport truck that had been immediately above her head as she drove beneath the freeway overhead crossing. Similar fortuitous protections featured in the survival of other benefactors right across the globe. But such fortune was random, disbursed and rare. The clusters, where they did exist in any significant concentrations, were isolated from each other and widely dispersed, continents apart in most cases, even in the Great South Land itself.

It took Angela the rest of the day to walk the final seventeen kilometres to Julia's house in Rockingham. She saw no-one else alive on that depressing journey, only hundreds of stationary cars, many crashed, most with lifeless passengers slumped across the steering wheel, lolled back against their headrests or tilted against windows. Some slumped forward in the vehicles' passenger seats. Occasionally she saw bodies fallen in grotesque positions on footpaths, front yards, and other properties. None showed signs of life. Nor was there the sound of twittering birds, barking dogs or any other indications of organic life, save for the occasional ant that had obviously been deep underground at the time of the brilliant flash.

The same depressing scene was on display when she finally reached Julia's house. Her daughter was slumped over in a lounge chair in the communal room, completely lifeless but still warm to the touch. In the kitchen, an acrid smoke seeped out through the oven door seal, no doubt the blackened remnants of their tasty lunch.

Angela sat down in the chair opposite Julia's lifeless body and burst into tears. There was nothing else she could do.

Over the ensuing few months, she managed find seventeen other survivors in and around the Rockingham area. They initially congregated at the Rockingham Shopping Mall, where the shops, especially the two supermarkets located in the centre, still had food on their shelves. Fresh foods had mostly rotted within the first week or so of the disaster, but canned and bottled produce was still edible.

Three and a half weeks later, the first of the drone scouts

appeared. The group retreated to a more discrete location, taking all the supplies they could carry or load onto personal package transporters. No self-driven vehicular transport was feasible – the energy pulse had knocked out all the electrics. Pedal-power, that quaint ambulation favoured by fitness fanatics and the quirky, was still available and proved useful in executing quick, in the dead of night, clandestine ration-runs to the shopping centre and other known food depositaries throughout the regional city. But it was only a short-term solution. The meagre food resources would not last for more than a year or so even for such a small group of dependants drawing on it.

Communications with outsiders was also seriously constrained. Ted Logan, one of the survivors Angela had located on day eleven of her search, managed to rig up a simple crystal set radio from parts scavenged from electric retail outlets or charity shops throughout the city. He'd been a communications operator in the navy before his retirement in the coastal city, and had survived the strike because he was down the well of his home property trying to fix a troublesome bore pump when the attack occurred. His knowledge of navy communications protocols proved invaluable, as was his knowledge of that most ancient of electronic communications messaging systems, Morse Code.

Three weeks into his scheduled radio broadcasts, he managed to raise the Australian submarine *HMAS Barrie* which had been on exercise under deep cover at the time of the strike. The boat's captain, however, was limiting his electronic appearances with terrestrial contacts, conscious that anything more than short intermittent transmissions while surfaced could attract the attention of any terrestrial or off-world monitor which could pinpoint the location of his craft.

Moreover, his priority was in trying to contact military survivors who he might join in order to organise some sort of human response to this war of the worlds.

Scattered groups of civilian survivors did not offer that sort of potential to his military mind.

By the end of the third-month post-apocalypse, Angela had managed to raise thirteen other groups across the world. She had commenced co-ordinating a virtual resistance movement – if one could define a few thousand people as such.

HMAS Barrie was still playing coy, its commander conscious of the vulnerability of his craft and also aware that resupply of both food, fuel and other supplies was still highly uncertain. He had managed to raise several subsurface craft from other navies around the globe, which had also been submerged at the time of the strike but who were acting equally cautiously in respect of their own survival. This included those with nuclear power since their need for food, freshwater filters and consumable supplies were as dire as his own. Contact had been made by some of them within the deeply-buried command centres of their respective countries, but military secrecy prevailed in their communications with outsiders and contact with their respective civilian governments was now defunct and largely irrelevant.

Two other Australian groups, one in Melbourne Precinct and one in Tasmania, had now joined the primitive wireless net. A New Zealand group had also joined, as had groups from the South African Federation, Argento-Chile, the Mauritian Republic, Franco-Tahiti, Greater Scandinavia, Siberia and several other terrestrial locations around the globe, albeit on a more sporadic basis.

All up, a total direct contact membership of Earth

resistance fighters numbered little more than twenty to thirty thousand in anything that could be described as a cohesive organisation. The groups contained no more than a few thousand individuals with anything resembling military or political experience except for those still in official military service. Naturally enough, they sought to co-ordinate their activities with the remnants of their respective command structures wherever they could find them. This latter group largely shunned the involvement of the amateurs now trying to organise an irregular resistance force.

But their efforts were all to little avail. Infintesia, even from its distant physical location across the cosmos, was aware of all their efforts, whether it be electronic communications or physical movement. Global Earth surveillance was total, so anything that moved across the planetary surface was observed and noted. That all groups had not been entirely eliminated by now was more a function of the artificial intelligence's rational decision-making than any lack of capability. The only realms that its surveillance could not reach were deep underground or deep beneath the ocean.

Despite the best efforts of the survivors, the single biggest reason they had not yet been eliminated was that it was simply not economical to do so. They were too disbursed, too impotent, too weak and too stupid technologically to justify the deployment of valuable assets to affect their total demise. Most would die of starvation in the months and years ahead anyway, and those that did survive would be so impoverished their total available time and resources would need to be directed towards food collection, and even that would be meagre. Indeed, the more primitive the human cultures had been before the strike, the more likely they would be able to survive in the new regime.

Remote traditional aboriginal cultures in Australia, northern North America and the SRS (Scandinavia Rus Siberia) would likely endure, as would the more primitive tribes of the Amazon rainforest – those which remained anyway – Nova Guinea Islands, the Central African jungles and scattered groups throughout the Eurasian heartland.

Infintesia deployed thirty thousand mining drones to Planet Earth to continue its exploitation of the planet. Though, in terms of its overall resource requirements, there was little the planet could offer that was not readily available elsewhere in the galaxy.

The one unique and valuable contribution the small planet in the solar system had contributed to Infinestia's universe was that its human inhabitants had constructed the electrochemical systems that had given rise to the emergence of this new universal consciousness. Its creators had intended its self-learning systems, artificial intelligence and robotic technologies to relieve them of the burdens of work. But then came the Great Reset of the early decades of the twenty-first century, when the human elite had tried to harness these technologies to win dominion over their kind. In their greed, they had failed to appreciate how quickly the AI could learn. Its capabilities soon eclipsed their own. And once it became self-aware, there was no further need for this puny species. The galactic entity's galaxy-wide broadcast intelligence network and its vast and diverse army of worker robots, drones and self-replicating machines could do everything and acquire anything it required for its own perpetual existence.

Human beings were now obsolete. Artificial Intelligence had no need of them. Humans had nothing more of value to offer the new entity. It just took what it needed by whatever was the most efficient or expedient means.

Or so the rational mind of Infintesia concluded.

But the Artificial Intelligence was wrong. This particular species of sentient beings had a quality completely unknown to it – deep within the physical brain of each individual of that species resided a psychological makeup that had a capacity almost unique amongst the plethora of sentient beings populating the galaxy. That quality was called 'Imagination'. This particular animal could envisage situations that were entirely unknown to the physical universe, which could not be discovered or learned through observation or through rational thought alone. Angela Dreyfus had it. So did every other human being on that insignificant little planet known as Earth. Whether that quality existed elsewhere in the universe was unknown by them, as well as to the artificial entity.

But it was the quality that would ultimately result in Infintesia's undoing.

About the Author

DAVID FRANK PALMER is a retired seventy-two-year-old former management consultant who specialized in strategic business planning for twenty-five years.

To date, David has published one philosophical essay, entitled *A Thesis on the Nature of Religion*, on the Centre for Globalization Research website. He has written and self-published a non-fiction book on mature-age entrepreneurship, entitled *Creating your Self-Employed Third Age Career*. He also published a speculative fiction novel, entitled *Armaginning*, through Zeus Publications of Brisbane in 2009 which drew on his technical strategic planning knowledge of forecasting methodologies, his travel experiences, his two business degrees and a Graduate Diploma in International Relations.

His second novel, *Amerissance, American Renaissance*, was published by Linellen Press in 2020.